INTO THE HAZE

BY: P.M. ARTHUR

First Printing: October 2018

Edited by Jaysie Meledeo
Cover design by Stefan Alekzandru (AZK)

ISBN 978-1-7328622-2-7
eBook ISBN 978-1-7328622-3-4

P.M. Arthur
www.pmarthur.com

Printed and bound in the United States of America

For my brother, Jordan, whom I'll never forget. The pain of loss almost halted this story, but the joyous memories gave me the strength to press on.

PROLOGUE

When Evan Jordan Miles was eight years old, he and his family had been in a bad car accident. He was the only survivor. As there were no other relatives to take care of him, Evan was placed into the care of an orphanage. He was so scared and felt incredibly alone. Everything happened so fast.

In the blink of an eye, his world as he knew it was changed.

When he was being brought to the orphanage, Evan kept thinking about his bed. When he had gotten out of bed that morning, he had gotten out of HIS bed. Completely unaware of the fact that when it came time to go to sleep that night, he would be sleeping in a foreign bed, in a foreign room, in a foreign place. Surrounded by nothing but the feeling of loneliness. The reality of what had happened was finally settling in and it was overwhelming little Evan.

By the time he arrived at the orphanage, he was a complete mess. He missed his mom. He missed his dad. He missed his little brother. The caretakers wrapped a blanket around him and brought him inside, sitting him on the couch. They hugged him and tried to calm him down, but they knew it was going to be rough for a bit. Everything was still fresh for him.

At that point, several of the other children in the place were lurking about to see what was going on. Some of the caretakers tried to shoo them back into their rooms, while others went to get some food for Evan. One particularly spry ten-year-old stood at the top of the staircase with her arms crossed, just staring at the mess that was Evan.

"Hey kid!" yelled the girl from the top of the staircase.

"Perri!" gasped one of the caretakers. "Get back to your room! He has had a rough day and your rudeness is not going to help."

"Let me show him around. He's an orphan now. Might as well let an orphan take him around and show him the place."

The caretaker looked at Perri cautiously for a minute and then smiled in defeat. "Okay, fine. But I expect you to be back in your room within the hour. And bring him back to me when your tour is finished. I mean it, Perri!"

The girl zoomed down the stairs. Her long, chocolate brown hair that had been pulled into a ponytail was flailing out of control. She abruptly came to a stop in front of the couch where Evan was still seated. She looked him over, noticing his short, unkempt orange hair.

"What's your name, kid?"

"E-e-v-van," he stuttered out between sniffles and stifled sobs. "M-miles."

"Good to meet you, Evan Miles. I'm Perri. Perri Jeane Pearson, at your service," said the girl, waiting to see if Evan was going to look up at her. "Look, kid. Things are going to be tough for a little while. You've just lost a lot. But the thing is, we all have. All of us kids here have been where you are now. We've all cried and cried and cried. It's okay. But, trust me, it's going to get better."

Evan wiped his eyes and sniffled a few more times before finally looking up at the girl who was standing in front of him. She was smiling at him and holding out her hand. He looked confused.

"Trust me, Evan. Everything is going to be okay. Just stick with me and I'll look after you. Then you're sure to be in tip-top shape." Perri winked at Evan and displayed a cheesy grin on her face. Evan returned her cheesy grin with a hint of a smile. "Now come on, let me show you around your new home. It's not so bad, really, once you get used to it."

Evan reached out and grabbed Perri's hand, and together they headed off on the tour of what would come to be his new home.

CHAPTER ONE

Day after day, the routine for Evan had consisted of the same thing. And, quite frankly, he was sick of it. He would wake up to the most annoying alarm, proceed to take a shower that would *always* turn cold before he was finished, put on the most ridiculous work uniform, eat the most bland breakfast, and then nearly be late to the most boring job in the world.

At the age of twenty-five, Evan did not imagine he would be sitting behind a desk and tethered to a phone all day, every day. His job was to sell jobs. The Company pretty much owned the majority of everything, which is why they controlled the jobs in the first place. People would call in because they needed work, and it was up to him to look over the list of available jobs and try to sell them one. Work was not free. Everything came with a price. The poor needed work, but the only way to get work was to buy it. If they could not afford to buy a job, they would be transferred to the Loans Division where they could take out a loan to buy the job. It was a vicious circle that Evan found himself a part of. He hated working for The Company.

While he was growing up, Evan never really knew what he wanted to do with his life. When people would ask him what he wanted to be, he never had a clear answer. He would always just shrug his shoulders and say that he wanted to do something interesting. That was the best he could come up with. So, his plan was to go to college and take a bunch of different classes with the hopes that something would stand out to him. Unfortunately, nothing ever did.

Like most people Evan's age, the only feasible way to get through college was to take out a contract with The Company. At the time, no one really knew what they were signing away. All they knew was that they would have their schooling paid for and a guaranteed job for five years afterwards. That was the contract. The Company would pay for college, but when a person graduated they essentially owned them for five years. To a kid going into college, what didn't sound good about free schooling and a guaranteed job for five years?

Evan's first sales call was a middle-aged man trying to get a job to provide for his family. He had just recently lost his wife due to illness, so they had a lot of medical expenses. And the contract on his previous job had just expired. Evan had never heard a grown man sob before, so it was definitely a new experience for him. He tried to calm the man down and tell him they would find him something. When he told him what was available, the man said he wouldn't be able to afford it. Evan looked down at his script and saw that he had to tell the man he could either be transferred to the Loans Division to take out a loan or do without. He felt that was really harsh.

That being his first call, Evan didn't want to screw things up, so he mentioned the Loans Division. The man got even more hysterical. Evan called for help from his supervisor. When his supervisor took over the call, he told the man in a very stern and very hateful tone that if he did not take out a loan, then he would be placed on a ban list in which he would never be allowed to take out job contracts again.

From that point on, Evan started counting down the days until his contract was over. He realized he had made a grave mistake by signing with that place. Evan had been sick of his life for a long time.

The only thing that kept him from going completely insane was his best friend Perri. She was the up to his down. The light to his dark. When Evan would see the worst part of a situation, Perri would always try to put a positive spin on things. She always remained level-headed, whereas he was nearly always overwhelmed. In truth, she mellowed him out. They'd been like that ever since they met as children.

* * *

Like Evan, Perri was also tired of the life she'd been living. However, she tried her best to maintain her calm and positive demeanor. She did not want to contribute to Evan's chaos when he got fired up about how awful things were. But she could not deny that she, too, wanted to get away from it all and start anew. Things had not turned out like she thought they would.

It was not the life she wanted, and she felt like a prisoner.

Unlike Evan, she always knew what she wanted to do with her life. She wanted to help people.

Since she was two years older than Evan, she decided to wait and start college with him at the same time. During that interim period, she stayed at the orphanage to help the caretakers out. That's when she further cemented her passion for helping those in dire need. Then she and Evan both took out contracts with The Company together and started college.

While Evan took a hodge-podge of classes trying to figure out what he wanted to do, Perri took a bunch of classes related to therapy, counseling, sociology, and psychology—basically anything that she possibly could take in order to find what area she wanted to specialize in. She developed a knack for each of those areas but found she preferred counseling. She liked listening and providing guidance to others in difficult times.

As someone who grew up through difficult times and was surrounded by countless others going through difficult times, her best friend especially, it was a no-brainer to Perri. It seemed that people always talked to her when they had problems, which made her feel like she had a natural gift of providing peace to others. As a matter of fact, she always considered Evan her first "unofficial" patient—from when they were kids, of course.

When college was over and the five-year job term began at The Company, Perri was placed in the Loans Division. Everyone who had a college-contract with The

Company was randomly sorted into a division at the start of their first day. There was a 30-day trial period to see if that person would work out in that division. If the trial was successful, they were locked into that division for the next five years, unable to move until the contract was fulfilled. If the trial was unsuccessful, another sorting was performed, followed by another trial period. That continued until the individual was found a divisional home for the next five years. Once the contract had been fulfilled, they had the option to create an official career contract with The Company, which gave them the choice of trying out other divisions. Or they could completely move on and out into the world.

Perri remained as positive as she possibly could at work. If she didn't, then she would be an absolute wreck–because the entirety of her customer base was comprised of people who were unable to afford jobs on their own, requiring them to take out loans to even afford to buy a job. How's that for irony?

But Perri, being the helpful person she was, would always make sure the customers understood everything they needed to know about the loans. And she would always let them know that everything was going to be okay as long as they immediately started paying off the loan when their job began. The sooner they rid themselves of the loan, the better. Her supervisors didn't particularly care for her verbiage, but they couldn't turn their heads from the fact that she had the best numbers in the division and the highest customer satisfaction rating.

That being said, Perri knew she had to get out of there as soon as possible. It was killing her to be there.

She tried to convince herself that she was helping people by giving them the best advice, but she knew that her very job was the opposite of helping people. She was technically an accomplice in making their lives worse. Forcing people who already didn't have any money to take out loans. It was truly despicable.

The only thing that kept her from going totally bonkers was Evan. And that was mainly because whenever she would start to think about finally unleashing her true feelings about that place, she would see how he was feeling and realize that he was having a much harder time. That would lead to her turning on her "counseling" mode, which always set her mind at ease because she was truly being helpful. And helping her best friend in the process. Calming Evan down was actually a therapeutic thing for Perri. It was odd in its own way, but getting Evan to relax and remember that everything was going to be okay was like Perri telling herself the same thing. Especially these days.

Evan and Perri spent a good chunk of their time together. They had been best friends for nearly two decades, and with no family in the picture for either of them, they were pretty much all each other had.

They typically got off work at the same time and would go to their separate homes to unwind first before meeting back up. They almost always hung out at Perri's place because it was more conveniently located within range of everything, and it was just all around cozier than

Evan's place. Not necessarily cleaner or tidier, just co-zier. Evan didn't mind. Like pretty much everything else in his life, he hated his bleak apartment, so any excuse to not be there was great for him.

It wasn't necessarily odd for Perri to come over to Evan's place, as they'd hang out there occasionally. But it was odd for her to come over there unannounced. She knew how Evan liked to have things planned out, and when they always planned to hang at her place, throwing a kink in that plan was like throwing a wrench right into the center of Evan's brain.

That's exactly what happened one evening as Evan was getting ready to head over to Perri's.

It had been a long day at work and, as usual, all Evan could think about was how much he hated everything about his life. Especially being stuck working for The Company. That usually created the downward spiral pattern that everything else followed.

Unbeknownst to Evan, his best friend also had a long day at work.

As Evan reached for his car keys to leave his crappy apartment for a few blissful hours, he heard a rapid knock on his door. He turned and stared in the direction of the frantic noise. Frozen.

No one ever knocked on his door.

"Evan, it's me. Open up."

It was Perri's voice. Evan felt like he was a computer starting to malfunction. Like a virus was taking over his system. He could feel his eye twitching and his hands shaking.

"Evan. I know you're freaking out. The silence gives it away. I'm sorry I didn't call first. But I need to come inside and we need to talk. Please open the door."

When the Evan-bot finally rebooted and regained his composure after a few seconds, he reached for the doorknob and opened the door to find Perri standing in the doorway.

"Uhhh. I dunno what's going on but come in, I guess," Evan mumbled out, as if he'd never spoken before.

"Relaaaax! It's not like I haven't been here before," she said as she walked through the doorway, quickly closing the door behind her. "But seriously. I've been thinking a lot about this and there's something we finally need to talk about."

Evan looked at her confused, eyebrows raised as high as they could go. "And that would be?"

"Leaving. I'm sick and tired of this place. I can't do it anymore. I know you hate it. It's all you talk about. I hate it, too. I've been holding it in for a long time and I'm done. I'm just done. I remember you used to have a plan to get out of here, and we haven't talked about it in a long time. I'm ready. Let's run away from this hell and never look back."

Evan's eyebrows dropped back to their normal level and a big smile formed on his face. He hadn't looked that happy in years.

CHAPTER TWO

*A*fter Evan had first arrived at the orphanage, he never really made any friends other than Perri. They'd hit it off basically ever since his first day there, when she had taken him on a tour of the place. From that moment on, he had sort of clung to her, and they'd become inseparable.

Perri was well known amongst all the other children, as she had been there longer than most. But Evan had become very introverted and did not like talking to anyone other than Perri. Everyone else usually made him nervous, whereas she made him feel relaxed.

Several months had passed since Evan had first arrived at the orphanage before he finally told Perri about what had happened to his family. They'd never really talked about their families. They'd always talked about everything but that subject. In that place, it was always a sore subject for most people.

But one day, when they were outside sitting on a bench going over schoolwork, Evan just sort of blurted it out. He wasn't sure why. He was thinking about his family a lot at the time and about how Perri felt like the closest thing he had.

"Perri, I was in a car accident. That's how I got here. That's how I lost my family." Evan was looking down at the ground, a solemn expression on his face. Perri was taken aback by the sudden change in topic from schoolwork. She listened attentively as Evan revealed his story to her.

He told her that his family would always take a trip every Saturday. His mom would come wake him and his little brother up to get dressed while his dad loaded up the car, having already packed the night before. They always had a quick breakfast and then off they went.

His dad would always surprise them by picking a new place to go every Saturday. Sometimes it was something simple like spending the afternoon at a new playground or going to see a movie in a different city. And sometimes it was more elaborate, like going to a big amusement park all day long or going hiking and camping out in the woods for the remainder of the weekend.

When they would get in the car to head out on their Saturday adventure, it would always be something new. Evan's dad would always give him and his little brother five chances to guess what sort of thing they were going to do that day. If they guessed correctly, they were able to pick where the family went the next time. They had succeeded a couple of times and were able to revisit a couple of favorite spots. But for the most part, their dad was always good about stumping them with a new surprise.

On that particularly unlucky Saturday, Evan and his little brother did happen to guess correctly. They were going to be spending the day on a boat trip on the river. Life jackets, canoes, everything. Evan's dad wasn't taking them to a big dangerous river with a really strong current or anything. Just one of the smaller rivers with a pretty tame current that he and his little brother would be more than capable of handling. Or so his dad had said.

Evan's mom was a bit nervous about the trip, but she tended to be nervous about most things that had the potential of endangering her boys. Evan had recalled his dad reassuring everyone that everything was going to be just fine.

And that was the last thing Evan had remembered hearing his dad say.

Right after that, their car had been struck by another vehicle, and when Evan had woken up, he was in an ambulance being treated for some minor cuts and bruises. The rest was history.

Evan finished the story with tears in his eyes. "We never made it to the river for our boat trip. I lost my mom and my dad and my little brother. Everyone died but me. And since I have no other family, I was sent here. To the orphanage."

Perri gave him a hug. "I'm sorry, kid. But just think. If you hadn't been sent here, then we wouldn't have met and become good friends." She flashed him a smile, and he smiled back.

"Yeah. That's a good way of looking at it," Evan said, while sniffling and wiping away the tears from his damp eyes. "Why do you call me 'kid' all the time anyway? You're barely two years older than me."

Perri let out a slight chuckle. "It's not just you, kid. It's what I call everyone. And I'm not sure. Maybe it's because I've been here longer than almost everyone, so I just feel like I'm older than everybody else." She paused and whatever joy she had on her face melted away as she looked down at the ground.

"I never knew my parents. Not really. I've been here since I was barely six months old."

She began to tell Evan the story of how she came to be at the orphanage. At least the story that was told to her by the caretakers over the years.

Perri's mother and father both died the day she was born. Her father had been out of town for work, and when he had heard the news that her mother thought she was about to have the baby, he set out on the first flight he could. That plane never made it. There was an accident with the engines and it had crashed, killing everyone on board. When Perri's mom had given birth to her, there were some really severe complications. The doctors had managed to save Perri, but her mother didn't survive. She had passed away during childbirth.

It was all sort of a freak accident that both of her parents lost their lives in separate ways that day—the day she came into the world. But, thankfully, she wasn't without anyone. Her mother's parents, Perri's grandparents, had been there. They had had a rough go of it for a little while. Losing their only daughter and their son-in-law on the same day. As well as taking in a newborn baby at their age. Unfortunately, all of the grief, pain, loss, and stress had taken a toll on them.

Six months later, Perri's grandmother had a heart attack and passed away. Trying to raise a newborn baby and deal with all of the grief was too much to bear at their age. Because of that, her grandfather didn't last more than a week after the death of his beloved wife. He, too, passed away.

That left a six-month-old baby Perri with no one.

Thus, she had been sent to the care of the orphanage. And that is where she'd been ever since. The caretakers had told her the truth fairly early on, rather than shield her from everything. They'd wanted her to know the truth sooner rather than later. So that she could own it and not live a life wondering where she'd come from.

Evan stared at her in disbelief. He thought his situation was rough, but at least he knew his family. Had all of those precious memories to hold onto. Perri didn't have anything. She had nothing but the orphanage. Then he thought maybe that was better. Maybe it was less painful.

"I'm sorry you never knew your family, Perri. That must be

tough."

Perri shrugged. "Yeah. I guess so. I wish I could've known them. Have some memories. But I do the best I can with what I've got. The caretakers have always been good to me. They're all I've known. I don't necessarily feel like they're family, but they're nice people. And now I've got you, kid."

Evan sighed. "Yeah, you do. So long as you stop calling me 'kid.' Perri, you're my best friend. You're my only friend, really. I lost my family. I don't want to lose you, too."

"Whoa, whoa, whoa. Where am I going? You going somewhere? You aren't losing me, kid. You're my best friend, too. Sure, I know almost everyone here. But, truthfully, I don't feel as close to anyone as I do to you. Friends need to stick together forever, ya know?"

That made Evan smile. He was afraid of losing the one friend he had and the thought was too much for him. "Let's make a pact, then. Let's do some sort of 'BFF' thing or something."

Perri wrinkled her forehead in thought for a few seconds before responding. "Hmmm. I think I have a better idea. We should have a codename."

"A codename? Just one?"

"Yeah! You don't want me calling you 'kid' anymore, right?"

"Definitely not. Especially if you call everyone else that. I'm your best friend, so I should get special treatment." Evan grinned after saying that.

"Well, 'BFF' is too common. Everyone uses it. Our codename can still be a pact that means 'best friends forever.' Just in a different way."

Evan looked at Perri in anticipation. "Well?"

"Give me a minute, I'm thinking!" Perri got up off the bench *and began pacing back and forth in front of it. Arms crossed, eyes closed, deep in concentration. After a few minutes, she stopped dead in her tracks. "I got it!"*

"Let me have it!"

"Pete!"

Evan just stared at her. "Uhhh…who?"

"Pete! That's our codename! Genius, right? Don't ask me how I even thought of it so quickly. I amaze myself sometimes." Perri flashed him a big smile.

"Pete. Pete. Why in the world would 'Pete' be our codename?"

Perri laughed. "Well, I'm glad you asked, Pete! For starters, it's a name and not just a random or weird word. So, if we write a note or a letter to each other and someone else sees it, they won't know who we're really talking to! It's so genius." Perri was clearly very proud of her idea. "And it's the same on the phone. If someone overhears me talking to you on the phone, they won't know I'm talking to 'Evan,' they'll just think I'm talking to someone named 'Pete!'"

Evan was in a daze, thinking about what he was hearing. Then he started to slowly nod his head. "Okay. Okay. That's pretty good. I think I like it. And having us both use the same name for each other keeps it simple. But what made you decide on the name 'Pete?'"

"Because. Like 'BFF,' it stands for something. And it basically has the same meaning. This is a pact. A promise that we're going to be best friends forever. And by using this name all the time, we'll ensure that we never forget this pact. P-E-T-E. Perri and Evan Together Eternally."

Evan thought about it for a minute. "You don't think people will think it sounds kinda…weird? I mean, we're just kids."

Perri scoffed. "Exactly. We're kids, so everything we do is weird. Besides, who cares what people think? We're the only ones that know what it means. Everyone else will only hear the word 'Pete.' But what do YOU think? Do you like it?"

"Honestly? I love it." Evan gave Perri a hug. "I don't know how I'd get through this without you, Pete."

"Me neither. We just gotta stick together and look out for each other, and we'll be just fine." Perri smiled at Evan. "We're more than just best friends, ya know. We're family now. And we can get through anything. It's you and me, Pete."

CHAPTER THREE

They made their way over to the couch and sat down. Evan was much more relaxed now, as he'd been waiting years to hear that Perri was also finally ready to leave their crappy life behind. She, on the other hand, was the opposite of relaxed. Sitting upright, stiff as a board, she just stared straight at Evan.

"Do you still have your plans of running away and starting over?"

Evan smirked. "Of course I do. I think about them all the time. Look at them almost every day. Making little adjustments here and there depending on my mood."

Perri looked down for a few seconds in silence before looking back up at Evan with her emerald green eyes narrowed. "Why haven't you left yet? I know you hate this place so much. I know how unhappy you are and have been for so long. Why have you just been sitting on your plans?"

"Why do you think? Because of you. We're best friends and you're all I've got. You're my family. If I'm going to leave and go start my life somewhere else, I'd rather you be there, too. So, I figured I would just wait until you felt like you wanted to leave as well."

"But what if I never wanted to leave?"

"Well, to be honest, I sort of forced myself not to

think about that too much. The thought of going without you stressed me out. And the thought of staying here forever…no. Not an option for me."

Perri knew there was no way Evan would stay there forever. Honestly, she had never planned to stay there forever either. But she had planned to at least finish out her contract with The Company.

Then all of that changed that morning.

"Well, you're right. We're best friends. We're family. I'm all you've got and you're all I've got. We're in this together. And I'm ready to go."

"Okay. But something happened. What was it? Tell me, Pete."

Perri explained everything to Evan. The events that had transpired earlier that day. The events that had finally pushed her over the edge and into the place that Evan had been in for years.

Several hours earlier, everything in the Loans Division had been normal. It was generally a well-oiled machine. There was a set amount of people designated to take the steady stream of calls of customers needing to fill out loan applications. And then there was another set of people who actually took those applications and processed them, sending them off to the appropriate division depending on what job the loan was for. The associates in the Loans Division rotated duties daily, so as to stay well-rounded on every task.

Today, Perri had been on phone-duty, and she also happened to be training a new recruit who had just begun her college-contract. Perri had gone over the usual how-tos of the phone system and the computer software, as well as the general "dos and don'ts" of customer service. Everything had been going smoothly until they received their first call after lunch.

That's when everything derailed.

Perri was used to people getting upset and emotional on the phone. With that job, it was a daily occurrence. She shared some of her techniques with her trainee, since she was pretty good about listening to people and calming them down.

That particular customer, however, was extremely hysterical. Perri went through her usual spiel of how everything would be okay as long as they paid the loan off as soon as possible. The customer began to get even more upset and actually angry with Perri, accusing her of not really wanting to help them at all. Perri told them it wasn't true and that she'd do everything she could to make the process easier for them.

The customer asked if Perri could lower the price on the job, effectively lowering the price on the loan. Perri explained to them that she didn't have the ability to do that, and the person went on about how badly their family needed the help. The customer kept gut-punching Perri by accusing her of not wanting to help and saying she was just like everyone else. Trying to take advantage of the poor.

Normally, she could shake things off, but that hurt too much. And just to prove them wrong, Perri told them she'd cover their loan out of her own pocket so their family didn't have to suffer anymore. She told them she truly cared about people, and she didn't want anyone to think she was taking advantage of them. She wanted to help in any way that she could.

Just then, the customer on the phone started to laugh and called Perri pathetic. At the same time, her trainee also let out a chuckle, then reached over and hung up the phone.

Perri looked at her trainee confused. Her trainee motioned to follow her.

She was led into the main conference room where half a dozen corporate executives were seated, staring at her. Her trainee told her it was all a setup. The customer, the trainee—it was all a ruse. They'd been onto her for a long time. They knew she had been misdirecting customers by trying to get them to hurry out of their loan contracts. That was the opposite of what The Company wanted. But since she led the Division in customer satisfaction ratings, they didn't want to make a big fuss. So, they setup a little operation to see just how far she was willing to go to "help" the customer out.

She fell straight into their trap.

For her big mess-up, she had two options. She could either extend her contract outright for three years and no longer speak with the customers, or she could finish out the remainder of her contract permanently on phone-duty—with the stipulation that during every call, she had to PUSH every customer to purchase loan extensions or be denied the loan.

All of the corporate executives wore venomous

smiles on their faces as she was forced to make an impossible decision.

When she finished telling all of that to Evan, he just stared at her in anticipation and said, "Well?"

"Well, what?"

"What did you decide? Which option did you choose?"

Perri scoffed. "Isn't it obvious? I couldn't, in good conscience, agree to force customers to choose between loan extensions or no loans. So, I went with the first option. Extending my contract and not taking customer calls anymore. No longer helping them."

That made Evan furious. Not at Perri. But at The Company. For forcing that decision upon her. It was as if he had just pieced the whole story together. "Our contracts were supposed to be finished in two years. And now you're saying that yours isn't gonna be finished for another five years? That's basically like starting completely over!"

Perri sunk down into the couch and looked down at the floor, a look of defeat on her face. "Exactly."

Evan didn't really know what to say. He felt angry. So angry at The Company, yet so horrible for how Perri must feel. He knew that she always kept it together all the time. And to see her sort of melt down like that usually meant she was really in a rough place.

Perri looked over at Evan, tears welling up in her eyes. "The only thing that kept me going at that place was the fact that I was helping them, Pete. I know that place is vile and what we do there is horrible. But the fact that I could talk to those people and reassure them everything was going to be okay…that helped me through it. Because I knew I was making a difference. I was still finding a way to help them. But that was shattered today. I can't start over. I can't do another five years there. Especially if I can't talk to them or help them. I'm not going to take part in this horrible life here any longer."

Evan reached under the couch and pulled out a folder with papers stuffed inside. He slapped it down on the coffee table and said, "Then it's time to go over our escape plans."

CHAPTER FOUR

*W*hen Evan and Perri were in their second year of college, they had received word that the orphanage was being shut down. Many of the caretakers had either passed on or were too old to properly run the place. Since The Company had grown so much over the last several years, it had been becoming increasingly more difficult to get help hired on anywhere. Unfortunately, that had also been affecting the orphanage. It had been harder for people to get jobs since The Company owned them all. And if people could afford jobs, they weren't going to go for a caretaker job at an orphanage. So, they had been forced to transfer the children to another orphanage in a different city.

Perri still periodically went by the orphanage to visit. Evan rarely went. Sometimes he would go with Perri, but he mostly stayed back at school while she went.

One day when Perri returned from her visit, she burst into Evan's room while he was looking over schoolwork. "Pete. The orphanage is shutting down."

"What?" Evan gasped as he jumped off his bed. "What do you mean shutting down? Why?"

Perri had an uneasy look on her face, and she started pacing back and forth. "Apparently, they just don't have enough help to run it anymore. A lot of them are gone now. And too old."

"Can they not hire new caretakers?" Evan asked.

"That's just it," Perri said, with a grim look on her face. "The

Company owns their jobs now. Which means—"

"—that they're pretty much screwed," Evan finished. "I thought The Company helped people find jobs, though? Shouldn't be difficult. The caretakers just need to let them know how badly they need help and I'm sure The Company will get someone in there. They're good at helping people. Look what they're doing for us. For kids going to college."

All the color left Perri's face. "The caretakers said they tried. The Company won't help them. They said if people can't afford to buy the jobs, then it's not their problem. The orphanage will have to turn the property over to The Company. They basically have no choice. There are no other options."

Evan had a look of confusion on his face. Then his expression slowly contorted into a fit of rage. He started having trouble breathing, as he was being overcome with anxiety and anger.

"Pete, you need to calm down," Perri said. "Getting yourself worked up isn't going to help anything. It's going to be okay. They're going to make sure the kids are transferred to another orphanage in a different city first. One outside of The Company's grasp. And the caretakers each have enough money to live off of. They'll be fine."

Evan sat on the bed and took a few deep breaths. Contemplating everything that was being told to him.

"I don't like it either," Perri said, walking over and putting a hand on Evan's shoulder. "I'm upset, too, but we can't let it bring us down. They did everything for us when we were kids and they helped raise us to who we are now. The least we could do is be there for them now. Anger won't help. So, come on. Look at me."

Evan looked up at her and gave her a fake smile.

"There he is." Perri smiled and pinched his cheek. "Now, I

need to get back to my room and study for a test, so I'll talk to you in a bit, okay? Remember, everything will be fine."

Evan nodded. "Sounds good."

Once Perri left the room, Evan began the first draft of his plans to run away.

When he had lost his first family, his first home, he lost a bit of himself. And, truthfully, he had wanted to run away even then. But then he had heard that his second home was being taken away and by none other than the people he thought he could trust. The people with whom he'd just recently signed away several years of his life. Perri might be able to shrug things off easily with her positive attitude, but not Evan. That was no life that he wanted. He needed to get out of there.

But he was going to have to play the slow game. It was going to take some planning and the most difficult thing of all. Patience.

CHAPTER FIVE

They both leaned forward as Evan took the papers out of the folder and began spreading them out all over the table. There were several sets of maps, checklists, and instructions. Each one was marked differently, clearly indicating priority and then backups. That way if one plan would not or could not work, they could resort to a backup plan. Some of the pages had red markings on them, already indicating that they were no longer viable options.

Perri studied the papers on the coffee table. "Alright, Pete. What am I looking at here?"

"Well, I've gone over a lot of different possible situations over the past couple of years. But I have finally settled on one that I think is the best option." Evan pulled out a map that had a big letter 'A' scribbled in the upper right corner. The map appeared to be a zoomed out map of their current city. The southern part of the map was a large grouping of trees and it had been circled. "This forest isn't far from here. Just a couple of miles. And if you can see on this map, there is a river that runs through it. This is where we need to go."

Perri looked at Evan, expecting him to reveal more. "Okay…and what do we need to do at this river?"

"This river just happens to connect to a small town

just a few miles east of here. I have already procured a small boat. All we need to do is get to the river, get in the boat, and then row, row, row, gently down the stream. We do that for a few miles and then we'll be there. We ditch the boat, head into town, start our new lives."

"Evan, that plan doesn't sound super solid," Perri said, looking a bit concerned.

Evan sighed. "Well, clearly I'm not done explaining. That was just the quick rundown of the plan. See all these papers? This is the good stuff. I have lists and instructions of things we need to do before we leave and things we need to do once we get there. Trust me, I've been working on this for a while. I've got it under control."

Perri stood up and began pacing back and forth. "My biggest concern is being somewhere so close. If this town is only a few miles from here, then is it really going to feel like running away? I figured if we were running away from this life, then we would be actually, ya know, running AWAY."

"I hear ya, Pete. Believe me. No one wants to run away from this hell more than I do. I've looked into it, though. This town might only be a few miles from here, but trust me, we're going to feel like we're very far away. It's a very small place and it is decades behind on technology. Once we get there, we're basically going to have no communication with the outside world. And it is super hidden away.

"Plus. We don't have to be there forever. It's just a

starting point. Because we're going to have to practically ditch everything we have before we leave. So, once we get back on our feet, we can leave and go a bit further just to feel more at ease if we want to."

Perri stopped pacing. "What do you mean 'ditch everything we have?'"

"Oh. Well, yeah I guess I hadn't gotten to that part yet. We're running away, Pete. Leaving this all behind to start over. So, I really think that's what we should do. Start over. From scratch."

Perri examined him. "But is it necessary?"

"Well, maybe not. But just think about it. If we don't leave everything behind, then we'll have ties back to this place. For instance, what happens when we don't show up for work? Our bosses will be calling us trying to figure out where we are. And when that goes on for several days, it'll get even more intense since we'll technically be breaking our contracts with The Company.

"That means they'll be trying to come collect our phones, our cars, and probably throw our credit cards into instant collections. They won't leave us alone. Best way to avoid that is to just leave it all here."

"This is crazy," Perri said. "Makes me feel like we're fugitives who are being hunted. All we're doing is just trying for a better life. We aren't happy here. We aren't doing anything bad."

"Well, you're not wrong," Evan agreed. "We, essentially, are fugitives. Or at least we will be. Sort of. Because technically we ARE breaking our contracts with them. They agreed to pay for our college in return for our employment. But in all honesty, I don't think The Company is going to bother with ACTUALLY trying to hunt us down. They have too many people to worry about. They're just going to be more focused on getting their property back.

"Once they find our phones and cars, and stop our credit cards, they'll realize we aren't anywhere to be found, and then they'll move on. We aren't worth it to them. They won't spend a dime to try to find us. They'll just move on to ruining someone else's life. And we can carry on our way towards our better life."

Perri's expression seemed to relax a little. "I suppose you're probably right." A slight grin formed on her face. "And just for the record, I'm not a big fan of this whole role-reversal thing we've got going on here, Pete. You're supposed to be getting the answers and advice from me."

Evan smiled. "Oh, come on. Cut yourself some slack. You're new to this. I've been at it for ages."

Perri nodded in acknowledgement as she sat back down on the couch. She leaned back and crossed her arms, thinking about the plan set before them. "So, if we can't drive…I'm guessing that means we have to walk to the forest."

Evan nodded.

"And we can't use our phones. So, that means we might as well turn them off and leave them here."

"Exactly," Evan confirmed. "Besides, the new town is so far behind the times that they wouldn't work out there anyway. No towers. No reception."

"And if credit cards aren't an option, then we're going to need some cash."

Evan mimed shooting a gun with his index finger and thumb. "Bingo. But I've got that covered. Been saving for this occasion. I've got plenty saved up. We'll be set for a while."

Perri studied Evan for a minute and then breathed a sigh of relief. "I'm so glad that you have this all figured out. I'm ready to get out of here, Pete. I'm not used to being in shambles like this. You know me, I'm usually more in control but—wait a minute. The boat. You said you already had the boat? Where is it?"

"Oh! I guess I forgot to mention. I've been back and forth to the forest a bunch. Just sort of going over the plan in my head and preparing for any potential disasters. Since some of my earlier plans fell through, I've been expecting this one to fail also. Anyway, I found a little nook just at the edge of the forest. Right by the river. That's where I'm keeping the boat.

"It's under a tarp. And the best part is, in all the times I've been down there I've never seen anyone else. I don't think anyone even goes to that part of the forest. So, it's safe where it is. I go and check on it every day. As a matter of fact, I haven't gone today. Wanna go see it?"

Perri jumped off the couch so quickly it made Evan gasp. "Well, yeah! What are we waiting for? Let's go!"

"Alright, but let's go ahead and leave our stuff here. Make it a sort of trial run. Since you're finally in on it, we might as well get a handle on what we need to do. I haven't been able to properly do one yet because I didn't want to do it by myself. In case something happened and I needed help." Evan looked at Perri and shrugged his shoulders. "You know how I can get if things go south."

Perri nodded and said, "Sounds like a plan." Then she placed her phone and car keys inside her purse and left it on the couch. "We'll leave it all here and go for a walk. You lead the way, Pete."

Evan placed his phone, car keys, and wallet on the coffee table. Then he went to the front door and grabbed a spare key that he had sitting on the entryway table. "Better take this so we can lock up our stuff and then be able to get back in."

He locked the door, and then the two of them set out on foot towards the forest. The forest that happened to have a river running right through it that connected to a small town where they were going to start their new lives. And at the edge of the forest, hidden in a little nook, was a small boat that would lead them towards their new home.

CHAPTER SIX

*E*van had had a lot of trouble sleeping the night before the big day. In just 24 hours, he and Perri would graduate from college and then the five-year term with The Company would begin. He thought it was going to be a good thing. Having college paid for and then a guaranteed job for five years.

But that was before he learned that those people weren't good people. They were vicious. They didn't actually want to help anyone. They were everything wrong with that place. That's why he started working on a plan to get out of there.

He wanted to run away. Sometimes he wondered if things would be better if his situation was different. He wondered if it would all be more tolerable if his family were still alive. If that horrible, stupid accident never happened. His parents probably would've helped him pay for college, and he wouldn't have had to take out a contract with The Company. That's for sure.

But it was no use thinking of things like that. They were gone. Never coming back.

Tears welled up in Evan's eyes. He stared up at the ceiling, thinking about where he wanted his new life to be. He knew it had to be far from here. A fresh start. But he'd never have enough money to go that far. He was going to be tied down there forever.

No. That was unacceptable to him. He wouldn't allow that. Just then, there was a soft knock at his door. Followed by a whispering voice.

"Pete? Are you awake?"

Evan got out of bed and opened the door. He saw Perri standing in the hallway. "What are you doing up?"

"I can't sleep. Figured I'd see if you were up, too."

Evan motioned for her to come into the room. They sat down on the bed. "Everything is gonna change tomorrow, Pete."

"I know. I can't believe it's already that time. And so begins our five-year term." Perri looked down at the floor, kicking her feet back and forth. "I'm sure it's gonna go by fast. It's not gonna be so bad. You'll see. I'm sure it'll be great. Plus, we'll both be there! And we might be lucky enough to be placed in the same division."

"I wanna run away, Perri," Evan said abruptly.

"What?" She looked up at him and saw he was looking back at her. "Run away?"

"Yes." Evan got up off the bed, walked over to the window, and looked out. "I don't like it here. My world has been flipped upside down ever since I was eight. Since they were ripped from me, Pete. The orphanage was fine and all. But then college came and I could never settle on what I wanted to do. I still can't. It's because I can't focus. Because this place has such a negative impact on me."

He turned around and looked at her. "And now we're locked into a five-year commitment with a place that is super shady. Who knows what is really going on there? Our days are probably going to be incredibly miserable. You know I don't do well with stressful or overwhelming situations." He went back over to the bed and sat down next to Perri. "But I'm working on a plan to get us out of here. We can run away. Start new lives somewhere else. We can be happy."

Perri had tears building up in her eyes, but Evan didn't seem to notice. "Why do you always do this, Evan?"

"Do what?" Evan said, taken aback.

"You always make everything seem so horrible. I guess our friendship over all these years hasn't been worth anything? Everything about this place is a negative impact? And you're not the only one who's lost something, you know. It's not fair that just because you have memories of your family that you assume you're the only one entitled to feel that loss and that pain.

"I've been there for you since the day we met, Evan. We're best friends. We've been through everything together. And now you say you just want to run away because you aren't happy here? Great. Nice. So much for 'Pete.'"

Evan was so stunned by the outburst from Perri that he was left momentarily speechless. But when everything sunk in that she had said, he thought for a minute and then finally spoke. "Of course our friendship is everything. You are everything to me! You are my best friend, Pete! That's why I said US. WE can run away."

Perri stared down at the floor, shaking her head. She wiped tears from her eyes but didn't say a word.

Evan continued, "And I never meant to act like you couldn't feel the loss of your family. But no, Perri, I'm not happy here! And you have known me all these years, so you should know that. I thought I could be happy until I realized what we'd gotten ourselves into with The Company. That's what set me over the edge. Look what they did to the orphanage and the caretakers. Can't you see they're terrible? Open your eyes, Perri!"

Perri jumped up off the bed, fury sweeping across her face. "My eyes ARE open, Evan. And they're looking straight at you. Someone who is unwilling to give things a chance. You saw one thing The Company did and you immediately think they're some evil thing bent on destroying your life? We haven't even started working there yet! Yes, they might be bad. But we don't know that! You ALWAYS do this. You ALWAYS assume the worst about everyone and everything. That's why you're unhappy. You just can't give things a chance! I've been keeping you calm for years and clearly that was a waste."

Now Evan was filled with anger as well, and he was shaking. "Well, you are way too naive about everything! Maybe I assume the worst, but at least I see things realistically! You live in a fairytale where everything has to be perfect and positive, and nothing can EVER go wrong for Perri! Grow up! Everything has gone wrong for you. Your mom and dad both died the day you were born! And your grandparents died within a week of each other when you were six months old! That's not a fairytale, Perri, that's a curse! Just face it, you're cursed!"

Perri had tears streaming down her face. Then in a calm and cold voice she said, "You're right. I am cursed. Because I wasted my life being friends with you."

She stormed out of the room and slammed the door shut behind her.

Evan threw himself down onto his bed and punched his pillow. Then he turned over on his back and stared up at the ceiling. As he laid there cooling off, he couldn't stop thinking about Perri. Regretting all the stupid stuff he said. But his mind remained unchanged.

He still wanted to run away. But Perri was the key to him leaving. He couldn't run away without her. He didn't want to. No. He would stay and endure the atrocities until she was ready to run away, too.

CHAPTER SEVEN

It didn't take them long to make the journey from Evan's place to the forest. Along the way, they went over their plans and what things they were going to pack up for the trip. They needed to make sure they had plenty of food and water. Since they were traveling a few miles in a row boat on a river, it was best to be prepared. And they needed to make sure they had some clothes. But not too much. They could only really take one bag each and then one bag of food.

"Okay, we're almost there," Evan said, speeding up his pace. "I have the boat stored just right...down..." Evan went pale when he reached the location where the boat was supposed to be. "...here."

Perri caught up to him and stared at the empty nook that once housed the boat. The nook was located just at the edge of the forest, with the river just a few yards away. All that was there now was a lonely tarp. "Evan?"

"I. This. What? No," Evan sputtered, and fell to his knees, tears in his eyes.

"It's gotta be around here somewhere, right? I mean, boats don't just go walking off on their own. And I doubt someone stole it. You said yourself that no one ever comes down here. I'm sure there's a logical explanation." Perri tried her best to sound positive, but she could tell that Evan was losing it more and more by the second.

"Perri. I was just here yesterday and it was here. It was fine. Everything was fine. This completely ruins our plans." Evan started breathing really rapidly.

"Pete, it's gonna be fine. We'll figure something out. If we have to find another boat, we will. That doesn't seem like it'll be a big deal. But you need to take a few deep breaths and calm down. You're getting yourself worked up."

Evan closed his eyes and did what Perri said. He took a few deep breaths. Then he stood up and looked around to examine the area. "This is a forest. With animals. An animal must have gotten over here and dislodged the boat. I had it wedged between these two rocks so it couldn't slide down into the river."

"See? Now that you've calmed yourself we can try to figure out what happened. We're literally right by the river. It had to have been something big, like a bear maybe? But it's perfectly possible that it slid right into the river after becoming dislodged. Which means it can't be too far from here."

Evan looked around. "You're right. Without someone to row the boat, the current isn't strong enough to carry it far. It should be close."

They walked down the incline from the nook that housed the boat until they reached the river. From there, it only took a few seconds before they spotted it not too far away.

"Hey, Evan, look!" Perri yelled as she reached back

and grabbed Evan's arm. She pointed in the direction of what appeared to be a small row boat resting motionless in the water.

They made a mad dash towards it. As they got closer, they could see that it came to a stop up against some branches that were sticking up out of the water.

"Come on, Pete. Let's go get it and bring it back to the nook," Evan said, stepping down into the water and wading over to where the boat rested.

Perri followed suit and, together, they pulled the boat away from the branches and back into the openness of the river. When they both hopped into the boat, they noticed that the oars were still resting at the bottom. They each grabbed one and began to row in sync with each other to make their way back towards the nook.

"See, Evan? I told you everything was going to be okay. You get so worked up. You can't let yourself get like that." Perri quickly reached a hand down into the water and then splashed Evan. She laughed when he was stunned by her aquatic betrayal. "You gotta relaaaaax. Like I've been trying to tell you forever."

Evan didn't say anything. He just kept rowing.

Perri's smile faded, and she put her focus back on the water and getting to the nook. Then when her guard was down, Evan quickly dropped his oar, formed a bowl with both hands, placed them down into the water, and delivered a devastating revenge splash. Evan smiled and burst out laughing.

Then Perri started laughing, too. "Well played, Pete. Well played."

CHAPTER EIGHT

*E*van had had a long day at work. Selling jobs was a lot harder than it sounded. Especially when having to listen to all of the stories of the customers. Evan knew theirs was a crappy situation to be in. His situation was really no better. Sure, he had a job, but at what cost?

He hated himself for what he was doing. Hated even being associated with that wretched place. But there was nothing he could do about it. Not right then.

Perri still wasn't ready to run away yet. At least not that he was aware of. After the big fight they'd had before graduation, Evan vowed to never bring it up again. Not unless Perri brought it up first. He knew that she would come around one day. That place was too bad for her not to. And he would be ready and waiting for her when she did. Because he would always wait for Perri. She was his family. She was everything to him.

Tonight was the night he was finally going to tell her.

It'd been a long time coming, but he was always just so nervous. And he was always worried that something was cursing him from being able to tell her. He had a feeling she felt the same way about him, but of course, he would never presume to have that knowledge. They'd spent so much time together over the past decade and a half that neither one of them really had had any other relationships. Sure, they'd talked about other people before, but deep down Evan only had eyes for Perri. And when he went to her place *tonight for their typical after-work hangout, he was going to tell her.*

He knew it wouldn't hurt their friendship either way. They were too close for that. They were all the other had. Sure, if she didn't feel the same way, then things would be horrible and awkward for a while. But they would be okay. And if she felt the same, then great. Things would only get better. And then maybe she'd finally agree to run away, and they could get out of there. Together. Really together.

* * *

As Perri was tidying up her place, all she could think about were the nerves she was feeling. Because tonight was the night she was finally going to tell Evan about how she felt.

It was something she had wanted to do for a while, but it felt like things were always standing in the way. She used to think that was a sign that maybe it wasn't a good idea. Maybe they weren't meant to be more than what they were. She was so close to Evan that she couldn't imagine ever having any sort of relationship with anyone other than him. He knew everything about her. And he had since they were kids. And she knew everything about him. They were all the other had. They were in this thing together. Basically, they were already partners, just without the romance aspect.

But she wanted that. And she wondered if Evan did, too. She felt like he did. She knew him pretty well. They definitely had a rough patch with the whole running away fight. That was brutal. But they got through it. Because that was what they did. That's who they were to each other. Everything. And they could get through anything.

Perri checked the time and noticed that Evan was late. She hadn't heard from him, so she tried to call him. There was no answer.

After fifteen minutes or so, she tried calling again. He still didn't answer. Evan was never late. He was always on time because he was a stickler for plans.

It worried Perri. She decided she was going to drive towards his place and see if something had happened along the way, so she grabbed her things and left.

* * *

Evan was so nervous. He didn't even realize that he was running late. He wanted to surprise Perri with some flowers, so he had to make an impromptu trip to a flower shop. When he realized what time it was, he reached for his phone to call Perri and apologize for being late. Then he realized he must've left it at home.

That was not good. She had probably tried calling him.

He hurried to get over to her place. When he noticed that her car wasn't parked out front, he didn't bother parking. He knew she would've left to try to see where he was. So, he drove in the direction of his place.

Halfway there, he saw flashing lights in the distance as traffic was backing up. It was at a standstill, and people were getting out of their cars to look up ahead at what was going on. Evan figured he would go ahead and follow along just to see. When he got out of his car and peered over the top to get a better look at the obstruction up ahead, his heart lurched.

There was a lump in his throat, and he starting shaking.

He saw Perri's car and another car smashed together in a big heaping, smoking mess.

"PERRI!" he shouted at the top of his lungs and began sprinting towards the wreckage.

When he got close, he was pushed back by the officers and firemen on the scene. He could already see someone on a stretcher being loaded onto an ambulance.

"That's my best friend! She's my family!" he shouted in a panic. Shaking profusely.

"Son, I'm sorry. But you can't come in here. You're welcome to follow the ambulance and go to the hospital. Do you know who we can contact for her, family-wise? Significant other?"

"NO. You don't understand. We are all that we have. I AM her family. I'm it. It's just us."

They studied Evan and then let him through. The officer shouted up at the paramedics in the ambulance.

"This one's with her."

One of the paramedics got out of the ambulance and looked at Evan. "It's not pretty, but you're welcome to ride back there with her. She's unconscious. It was a nasty wreck."

Evan thanked him and climbed into the back of the ambulance. He was horrified at what he saw. It caused him to burst into tears. He sat down next to his friend and took her hand into his own.

"I'm so sorry, Pete. I'm so sorry I was late. This never would've happened if I was on time."

He thought about the fact that if only he had kept his feelings suppressed like before, then Perri would be fine. All of those things happened because he wanted to tell her how he felt. He really was cursed. Or at least they *were.*

Maybe they weren't meant to be together after all.

He kissed her on the forehead. "I love you, Perri. I wish I could tell you for real. But maybe it's just not in the cards for us."

CHAPTER NINE

They had only been in the boat for a couple of minutes, as the distance they needed to travel was very short. However, they failed to realize that the current was getting a little stronger the closer they got towards the nook.

When Evan grabbed his oar again and put it back in the water, he wasn't prepared for the increase of the current. His grip was too relaxed, and the oar was wrenched from him. He turned and looked at Perri.

A look of confusion and concern swept over both of their faces.

"Evan, what happened?"

"I don't know. I just went to row and I lost my grip, I guess. Is it just me or does the current feel a little stronger?"

Perri looked down at the water. "Yeah, it does seem to be stronger. But we're about to pass the nook now. You ready to stop and put the boat back?" She looked up at the sky and then around at the forest. "It'll get dark soon and we still have to make it back to civilization."

Evan's eyes were transfixed on something up ahead in the distance. His brow was furrowed, as if he were deep in thought. "Yeah, you're probably right...dark soon...need to get back..." Evan trailed off, as if he wasn't completely paying attention. "Hey, Pete, do you see that?"

Perri looked at Evan and then tried to turn her eyes in the direction he was looking. "See what? All I see is the river."

Due to the increase in current and the fact that they didn't stop, they had passed by the nook completely.

"No. Something is weird about the air up ahead." Evan seemed to be a bit nervous. His breathing had started to become more rapid.

"Calm down, Pete. You always worry about noth—wait, I think I see it."

"I told you!"

Perri leaned forward and squinted her eyes to try to get a better focus on what the river was carrying them towards. "It reminds me of the way the air looks above the road on a hot day. Like some sort of heat haze—all wavy and distorted. How is that possible when it's not even hot outside?"

"Yeah and not to mention it's above water. Whatever it is, it gives me the creeps. We should turn around and go back. It's probably just some chemicals in the water that are moving up into the air. We don't need to be anywhere near something like that."

Just then, they picked up speed. The boat started moving faster towards the mysterious sight.

"Evan? What is happening?" Perri was getting nervous and she was usually the more level-headed one.

"I don't know! It feels like we're going downhill but we're not! We've gained so much speed. That thing is sucking us in, whatever it is!"

Perri panicked. "Evan, let's just jump out of the boat and swim back. We can get another one! I don't know what's going on here, but I'm honestly a little freaked out."

Evan's expression was eerily relaxed. His eyes were glazed over, and his voice became soft and mellow. "It's weird. I know we should jump out, but something about it makes me feel like I don't want to. You know what I mean? Just look at it."

Perri stared at Evan, even more freaked out by his sudden change in demeanor. Then she looked back towards the thing they were being drawn into.

She felt a sense of calm wash over her. She, too, became relaxed. Her eyes glazed over as they stayed transfixed on the mystery in front of them. In a soft voice, she said, "You're right. Now I don't feel like jumping either."

Evan reached out and grabbed Perri's hand, squeezing it tightly. They closed their eyes right before they crossed into the haze that floated mysteriously above the water.

When they passed through it, the boat skidded to a stop, as it was no longer on water but on dirt.

They opened their eyes.

"Uh, Perri?" Evan called out to his friend, but she was motionless, mouth gaping open. "Perri!" This time Evan nudged her. She snapped back to reality and looked at him.

"What just happened, Evan?"

"I…honestly don't know. But look around. We're in the same spot…it's just…"

"…there's no water," finished Perri.

Evan eyes were opened as wide as they could possibly be. "Did you…feel that? When we passed through it?"

"Yeah," Perri said. "It felt like my skin was burning and then freezing at the same time."

"And my head," Evan said. "It felt like I got shocked by a massive amount of electricity. My head is spinning a bit. I need to get out of this boat." Evan got out and stood on what should have been a riverbed. "Pete. How is this not water?"

Perri was still in the boat. Stunned by everything around her.

She looked at the sky, the trees surrounding them, then finally looked over at Evan and the ground he was standing on. "Maybe it dried up?"

"That doesn't make any sense. We should at least be standing a couple feet deep if that was the case. We're at the same level we were before we passed through that…thing." Evan pointed towards the mysterious air disturbance that they just came through.

Perri turned around and looked at it. She no longer felt a sense of calm staring at it. "What do you think it is?"

"I'm not sure," Evan said, walking towards it. "Whatever it is, we should stay away from it."

"But look, Pete. I don't think it's working the same as it did a few minutes ago. It's not pulling us in. And it made us act weird when we looked at it before. I don't think it's doing that now." Perri got up out of the boat and walked over to it. She reached her hand out to touch it.

"Perri, stop!" Evan yelled as he grabbed her and pulled her back. "What the heck are you doing?"

"I was just going to see if it did anything."

"We don't even know what this…haze thing is," Evan said. "We need to figure out what happened. It's going to be dark soon, so we don't have a lot of time. Let's get the boat back to the nook and get back to my place. We can discuss theories on the way. I don't want to be stranded down here."

They grabbed hold of the boat and started dragging it towards the spot where the nook was located. Once they reached the location, they saw that there was no nook. No opening in the side of the hill at the edge of the forest.

It was as if it had never been there.

They exchanged worried glances, dropped their grip on the boat, and sprinted out of the forest.

"Any guesses? I'm all ears," Evan said in between breaths while running.

Perri shook her head. "No. First the river. Now the nook. I'm too afraid to look at anything else. Let's just hurry and get back."

They made it back to Evan's place in record time. Once they got there, Evan put his key in the lock, but it wouldn't turn. He looked at Perri, who was still panting from the exhausting, anxiety-ridden run.

He tried it again. Still nothing.

Feeling anxious, he slowly raised a hand up to the door and knocked.

Someone came to the door and asked if there was something they could do for them. Evan asked them how long they'd lived there, and they said they'd been there for several years. He thanked them and they closed the door.

Evan's face was white, devoid of color.

He and Perri left the building and made their way to the sidewalk outside. They remained quiet for a while, both of them silently pondering what was happening.

"Time travel?" Perri threw her arms up in the air. "Am I ridiculous for even suggesting it? I mean, what the heck is going on around here?"

"Time travel. I guess that could explain the river, and the nook, and the people living in my place..." Evan said, pacing back and forth on the sidewalk. "But hang on. No, that doesn't make sense. If we traveled in time and the river was dried up or something, then why was the ground so high? No, this is something else. And the nook didn't look like it ever existed. Look around, this looks almost just like our time. Nothing looks futuristic. Or ancient."

Perri looked at the buildings that lined the street. And the cars that were driving by. They did resemble everything that was familiar to them. "This hurts my brain, Pete. What do you think, then?"

"I bet if we look at the date, it'll be the same date. I don't think we time traveled at all." Evan walked over to an older man sitting at a bus stop and saw he was browsing on a smartphone. He asked the stranger what the date was. The man shot him and Perri a suspicious look and then laughed. When he told them the date, Evan thanked the man and then turned to Perri. "See?"

Perri looked concerned and confused. "But I don't understand, then. What happened?"

Evan looked around again and then right back at Perri. He looked her right in her emerald green eyes and said, "Pete. I'm pretty sure we're in a different universe."

"Different universe?!" Perri yelled so loudly that people nearby stopped and stared at them.

Evan awkwardly smiled and waved at those around him who were still staring. Then he looked back at Perri. He grabbed her by the hand to lead her away and started walking down the sidewalk. "Think about it. When we passed through The Haze, we came out in a place that was similar but different. We thought we just went through a weird thing in the air. But that weird thing must be some kind of doorway to another dimension. A parallel universe. An alternate reality. And it brought us here."

Perri just kept listening. Waiting for Evan to continue.

"That explains why the river wasn't there. Why the nook wasn't there. Why someone else was living in my place. Because in this universe, that isn't a river. There is no nook. And I never lived in...that...place...." Evan trailed off. Then he stopped walking.

"What is it, Pete?" Perri stopped, too, and noticed

Evan staring at the ground, deep in thought. "Something just caught your attent-" then Perri gasped. "Oh my God, Evan!" Her eyes widened. "Different universe. Our families. Us."

Evan nodded. Then he looked at her. Tears in his eyes. "They might be alive here, Perri."

Perri studied him. "What do we do? Where do we go?"

"I'm not sure. We don't have our phones, so no internet access to search. It's too late to go to the library. Even in this universe, I'm sure it's closed by now."

"I wonder if the orphanage is here," Perri said. "Maybe in this universe, The Company didn't cause it to get shut down. I bet we could go there and check. You know the caretakers always had phone books lying around."

They made their way to the orphanage and, sure enough, it was still there. Still open. When they knocked on the door, they were greeted by a couple of familiar faces. Caretakers they recognized. But the caretakers didn't seem to recognize them. That seemed to indicate that neither of them had ever gone there. It filled them with hope.

Perri asked if they could borrow their phone book. When they thumbed through it, they found what they were looking for.

Evan's parents. He started crying.

Perri hugged him. "They're here, Pete! You can go see them if you want to. But it's pretty late. I know you're probably super anxious to go see them now, but maybe we should try to get some rest, and you can go see them first thing tomorrow? We've kinda been through a lot today."

Evan smiled. "Yeah. You're right. First thing in the morning. I can't believe it. This seems like a dream. The Haze brought us to a universe where my parents are still alive."

"I wonder if that means the car accident never happened at all! They're all safe, Evan. Your parents and your little brother."

Evan stared at her. "What do you mean little brother?"

Perri chuckled and said, "Good one, Pete."

Evan was serious. "Good one? Perri, what little brother? I don't have a little brother."

CHAPTER TEN

Perri felt her chest tighten, as if someone was stepping on it with a metal boot.

"That's not funny, Evan." She looked into his navy blue eyes and saw that his pupils were tiny. Not dilated, as if he were lying. And he wasn't flinching, either. He was telling the truth. Or at least he thought he was. He didn't think he had a little brother.

But Perri knew better. Perri KNEW for a FACT that Evan had a little brother. "What is going on with you?"

Evan grabbed his head, wincing in pain. "I don't know what you mean. But my head is really hurting, Pete. It has been since before we got here. I didn't say anything because I thought it was just a little headache. But I really don't feel well."

"Something's wrong. Evan. You have a little brother. You just can't remember."

Evan couldn't pay attention to what she was saying. He just kept holding onto his head.

Perri wondered why she wasn't being affected but he was. Something about this universe was having an adverse reaction on his brain. It was causing him to lose his memory. Would she be next? Was she going to lose something?

"Evan, I think we need to get out of here. We need

to try to get back home," Perri said.

"I don't think I can go anywhere right now, Pete. My head hurts too badly. I think I just need to…"

"Evan!" Perri called out to Evan, but it was no use. He had passed out.

The caretakers helped her move him to a spare room and onto a bed. They offered to allow them to stay for the night, but they requested they be out first thing in the morning. They weren't entirely comfortable with a couple of strangers around all the children. Perri assured them that they'd be gone first thing in the morning and that they didn't have anything to worry about.

One of the caretakers insisted upon sitting watch outside the room. Like a prison guard. They said it was for the children's safety. Perri smiled and wasn't about to argue with that.

When she awoke the following morning, she saw that Evan was stirring in the bed. She had slept on the floor with some blankets and pillows because she wanted Evan to have the most comfort. Since he was clearly experiencing something unusual. Evan rose up and looked around the room.

"Good morning, sleepyhead," Perri said.

"Good morning," Evan returned, with a big yawn. "Where are we?"

"We came to the orphanage last night, remember? Your head was hurting pretty badly and you passed out. The caretakers were kind enough to let us sleep here."

Evan considered that for a moment. "I do vaguely remember that. And last thing I remember is something about a brother?"

"You still don't remember him, do you?" Perri asked.

Evan shook his head. "It's weird, Pete. It's like, I know there's something that's supposed to be there. Like you said. But I have no recollection of having a brother."

Perri's face was contorted with worry. "Well, how is your head? Do you feel any better?"

"I do, actually," Evan replied. "Right now, anyway."

"Good," Perri said, relaxing. "Now we need to leave here and figure out what our next move is."

"Oh! Did you look in that phone book for your parents?" Evan asked.

Perri laughed. "What for?"

"To…see…if they're alive in this universe? Like we did with mine?"

Perri shrugged. "Well, I guess I can. But the reason we checked for yours was because they're not alive in our universe, Pete."

Evan's eyes narrowed. "Yeah…?"

Perri let out a snort. "What, Pete?"

"Perri, do you think your parents are still alive in our universe?"

"Think? What kind of question is that? Of course they are!"

Evan's eyes widened. He realized that must've been how Perri felt last night when talking to him. "Perri, is your head hurting?"

"Nope," she said, feeling her head. "Actually, it

kinda does feel sore. Ya know, like when you wake up after having gone to bed with a bad headache?"

"Did you go to bed with a bad headache?"

"Well, no. But I must've had a doozy in my sleep."

"Pete. I think you've been affected now, too. Your memories. You've forgotten what happened to your parents."

Her mouth fell open and she threw a hand to cover it, gasping in the process. "Evan. I can feel it. Like you said earlier. Something that's supposed to be there, but it's not." She looked down at the floor, eyes welling up with tears. Then she looked back up at Evan. "My parents aren't alive back home, are they? In our universe?"

Evan got down from the bed and put his arm around her. "I'm sorry, Pete. But no. They're not."

She sniffled. "We must've gone through some sort of psychological shock or trauma when we realized we came to an alternate universe. Maybe that's what caused the weirdness with our memories. They're probably just suppressed. I'm sure they'll come back. This whole thing is messing with our heads. Once we get home, I'm sure it'll correct itself."

"You're probably right. But let's try to find out if your parents are here. Then we can pay a quick visit to both of our families."

They asked the caretakers if they could look at the phone book one more time before leaving. When they scanned it, they found Perri's parents.

There they were. Alive and well. Now they had the addresses for both sets of parents. They copied them

55

down and off they went.

Evan and Perri discussed how they were going to play it. They had to take into consideration that there was probably an alternate set of themselves in this universe. And it would be way too weird to come into contact with one's self from a parallel reality. They figured that if they both existed in this universe and both parents were alive, then the two of them probably never met and became friends. Having never gone to the orphanage as children. Meaning their parents wouldn't know who the other was.

So, Evan would knock on the door of Perri's folks' house, and Perri would knock on Evan's. And when they answered the door, they would simply ask "Is Evan home?" or "Is Perri home?"

That would clear the air as to whether they would run into their alternate selves. They thought it was a good idea but later realized some things weren't taken into consideration.

They went to see Perri's mom and dad first. Evan went and knocked on the door. Perri stayed a couple houses away down the street, watching from a distance. She saw her mom answer the door and her heart dropped down to her feet. She had seen a picture of her before. But there she was, in the flesh.

Next thing she knew, her mom was shouting and then she slapped Evan really hard across the face. Evan turned around and slowly made his way back. His face was beet red and he looked as though he'd just shamed an entire village.

Perri raised her hands. "Well, what the heck was that?"

"Apparently you don't exist in this universe, Perri."

"What do you mean? What did she say?"

"She just said she didn't have a daughter. And how dare I have the gall to come snooping around."

Perri looked in the direction of the house. "I should go over there and meet her. Get a better look. And I didn't get to see my dad."

Evan shook his head. "Maybe this wasn't such a great idea. We don't know these people or what their situations are over here, Pete."

"Well, shouldn't we at least pay a visit to your parents? So that you can see them?"

"I don't know. I want to, but I'm feeling like we shouldn't." He thought about it for a minute. Then he sighed in defeat. "Okay. Same plan is in effect. You go to the door first. If it goes smoother than this, we'll meet. Otherwise, we're aborting like we did here."

When they got to Evan's house, he felt his insides swell with excitement and nervousness. It was the same house he grew up in. He was surprised they never moved.

While Perri went to the front door, Evan found a tree across the street to hide behind. She knocked on the door, then turned around to check and see if Evan was looking. The door opened and she heard a familiar voice say, "Hello, can I help you?"

Perri froze. She turned back around slowly until she was facing the source of the voice.

The person standing in the doorway had navy blue eyes and dark orange hair.

Across the street behind the tree, Evan started breathing rapidly. He couldn't believe his eyes. He was seeing an alternate version of himself. It made him queasy and he ended up retching on the grass. Then he looked back up to see Perri just staring blankly at the alternate Evan.

"H-hi," Perri said, shyly.

This version of Evan was unlike the one she knew. For starters, his hair was neat and tidy rather than un-kempt. He also had a much different persona about him. Whereas her Evan always seemed so anxious and nega-tive all the time, this one exuded positivity and confi-dence. He looked as though he were ready to take on the world. He looked so happy.

Perri snapped back to reality and realized she must have been staring at him for an inexcusably lengthy amount of time.

The alternate Evan smiled at her and asked again with a chuckle, "Can I help you with something?"

"I'm so sorry," Perri blushed. "You just reminded me of someone. But I think I might have the wrong house. Bye." She turned quickly and dashed as fast as she could away from the house. Completely passing the tree across the street that her Evan was hiding behind.

The alternate Evan watched as a seemingly crazy woman ran from his house. He laughed to himself and then went back inside.

Evan came out from behind the tree and ran after

Perri. When he finally caught up with her, they were two streets over and out of sight of the alternate Evan.

Evan laughed. "Well, that was weird."

Perri was still red in the face from embarrassment. "This whole thing is weird. I never expected you to answer the door. Or him. Whoever that was. I guess we know for sure you exist over here."

"Yeah, that's true. I was hoping to see my parents though. Did you happen to see a glimpse of them over his shoulder or anything?"

"To be honest? All I was paying attention to was him. It was so weird, Pete. He was you, but he was so different. He looked so..."

"Happy?" Evan said, his voice somber. "Yeah. I probably would be, too, if my life hadn't been flipped around. That guy didn't go through the pain I went through."

Perri couldn't think of what to say.

"Don't forget, Perri. The whole reason that got us into this mess was wanting to run away. Because of how unhappy we were with our lives. Remember? That guy. That Evan? That's who I want to be. I want to be that happy. I'll never be that happy at home. We wanted to run away and start a new life. Well, look around. Maybe we should just stay here." Evan reached up and grabbed his head, wincing as if in pain.

"What is it? Is your head starting to hurt again, Evan?"

Evan nodded.

"I think maybe we should get back home, Pete.

Something isn't right about this pain you're experiencing. We still have our plans. Once we get back to our universe, we can load up all our stuff and continue on with our plan like we intended to."

Evan nodded in silent agreement.

"Do you think you can make it back to the forest?" Perri asked.

"Yeah. I'm fine. It was just a short burst. Probably just a little residual pain from whatever happened last night. Let's go."

They made their way back to the forest, discussing everything they had experienced in the short time they had been in that parallel universe. They also wondered how long The Haze had been there. And how many others had discovered it before them. They wondered if that's where some missing persons cases ended up. Maybe people somehow stumbled upon The Haze just as they did and then crossed over into this universe. There would be no way for people to ever know for sure.

It was a rather unsettling thought.

When they reached the edge of the forest where the nook was supposed to be, they saw their boat was right where they had left it the night before. Knowing they would be emerging back on the river in their universe, they grabbed hold of the boat and dragged it.

They could see The Haze up ahead of them. As they started getting closer, they felt their feet moving faster against the ground. As if they were being forced into a run.

They lost grip of the boat, and it skidded to a stop

on the dirt behind them as they were forced forward.

"Perri! I can't control my legs! It's dragging us in again!"

"I know," Perri said in a calm voice. "Do like you did yesterday and look at it, Pete. It'll calm you and everything will be fine."

As they were involuntarily running towards The Haze, Evan looked directly at it and felt that sense of calm wash over him. Perri reached out and grabbed his hand. They closed their eyes as they passed through it.

They both experienced a sudden simultaneous burning and freezing sensation over their bodies, coupled with the feeling of an electric shock.

When they came out the other side of The Haze, they were expecting to be standing waist deep in the river, but instead they were standing on a metal floor. The area was filled with light. Above them was a glass dome. All they could see around them were glowing trees–the source of the lights.

"Pete. Pete! PETE! EVAN!" Perri was shouting, in a complete panic. Whatever bit of level-headedness she usually had was gone in that moment.

"I know, Perri," Evan said, unusually calm. "It would appear The Haze is not a connection from our universe to the previous one. It must be some sort of hole connecting multiple universes. Maybe even all of them. Every universe. I have no idea where we are. Or how we're getting home."

CHAPTER ELEVEN

They looked around at their marvelous surroundings. Everything was so resplendent. It was beautiful, yet terrifying.

Perri dropped to the hard metallic surface on her knees with a thud. She was sobbing. "What've we done, Pete? Where are we? What do we do?"

Evan felt horrible. He hated seeing Perri like that. Usually he was the one in distress and she was his anchor to serenity. He was pretty scared and concerned about their current situation as well. But seeing Perri like that made him realize that he needed to be her anchor. He needed to be that for her like she always had been for him.

Evan leaned down and said, "Hey. It's gonna be okay." He flashed her a smile and waved an arm in the direction of their surroundings. "Look around, Pete! Look at how beautiful this place is. It may not be our universe, but it's something different. Something we're lucky to see. Why not explore and see what it has to offer?"

Perri wiped her eyes and looked around. "I guess it can't hurt. But it looks like we're in some sort of dome. What do you suppose this place is? It's a far cry from the forest on our universe."

"I might be able to answer that question," spoke a woman's voice from nearby.

The two of them turned their heads quickly to find who the voice belonged to.

They saw a middle-aged woman dressed in long, flowing silver robes walking towards them. She bore a smile on her face as she approached them.

"Well, hello, and welcome to our universe." The woman bowed.

Evan and Perri looked at each other, then got to their feet and awkwardly returned the woman's bow. Perri gave an uncertain "Thank you?"

"Who are you? What is this place? How do you know we're from a different universe?" Evan blurted out.

The woman chuckled. "Don't worry, I'll answer your questions. But first thing's first. How are the both of you feeling? How are your heads?"

Evan and Perri didn't even think about the headaches. They reached up, felt their heads, and shrugged their shoulders.

"I feel fine," Perri said.

"Same here."

The woman studied them for a minute. "Not yet, I see." Then she smiled. "Okay. Well, follow me and I'll explain."

Evan and Perri looked at each other and nodded in silent agreement. Then they followed behind the silver-robed woman.

After walking a short distance on the metal pathway

through the forest of luminous trees, the woman stopped in front of a small building. She pulled a small device out of her pocket that resembled a pen. She held it above her hand and clicked it. Just then, an imprint of what looked like a clock appeared on the back of her hand. Almost like a tattoo. She held it up to the door and it slid open.

They followed her inside, and she guided them to a room with some chairs and a couple of small beds. "Please sit," she said, pointing to the chairs. She took a seat on one of the beds.

Evan and Perri looked at her, waiting for her to speak. The woman studied the two of them carefully.

"To answer your first question," she said, "my name is Tillia. But everyone calls me Tilly. I am a scientist and this is my facility. And I know you're from another universe because you two aren't the first ones to come through UnFor."

Evan and Perri gave each other looks of confusion, then Perri looked back at Tilly. "I'm sorry. UnFor? You talking about The Haze?"

"Yes," Tilly answered calmly with a smile. "That is what we call it. UnFor. It has two meanings. Scientifically, it is short for 'Universum Foraminis,' which is Latin for...well, 'universe hole.' But also, we think anyone who travels through it is *unfor*tunate." She stifled back a small chuckle after that last sentence. Perri and Evan didn't laugh. "We scientists here like to have jokes, too, ya know. But that's irrelevant."

"Yeah," Evan agreed. "What we all call the mysterious thing that transports us to different universes doesn't matter. What I want to know is how it works. You said you're a scientist and others have come through before us. So, you must have been studying it, right? Is that what this place is all about?"

Tilly had an uneasy look on her face. "Well, not exactly. It is and it isn't." She looked from Perri to Evan. She could tell they weren't pleased with her answer. Particularly Evan. "You see, we first discovered it many years ago. When we were transforming this forest into what you see now. We're a team of dendroluminologists. We study trees and the lights associated with them. Their effect on the environment."

Evan and Perri stared blankly at Tilly.

"I can tell by the looks on your faces that this sounds foreign to you. Understandable. Given the few people we have met thus far from other universes, we have learned that our trees have unique qualities. Regardless. When we discovered UnFor, we could tell right away that something was not quite right about it. It was a fascinating phenomenon. We kept an eye on it every day during our work on the forest, seeing if it was going to change or do anything. Then one day a man just came out of it. We were astonished."

"What did you do? What did the man say?" Perri asked, sitting on the edge of her seat.

"Well," Tilly continued, "we asked where he came from. It was clear he was from somewhere far different based on the looks he was giving us and his surroundings. Not unlike the looks you two had on your faces moments ago. He explained that he had just lost his job earlier that day and that he had gone through a messy divorce weeks prior. He was down on his luck and had gone out to relax. To get away from it all. He said next thing he knew he was being sucked into something he couldn't quite make out. Then he appeared here."

Evan got up from the chair and stretched his legs. Then he walked back and forth around the room. Shaking his head. "Did you or any of your scientists ever try to go through it? Ever get sucked into it?"

Tilly shook her head. "No. It doesn't work for us. But for that, we think we have the answer. You see, the other visitors who've been here have shared similar experiences. They were trying to escape something or run, get away. That's when they were sucked in. If I had to wager a guess, the same goes for you two?" Perri nodded. "And that's why it hasn't worked for us," Tilly continued. "We're all happy here. We have no reason to leave. We don't want to." She smiled and shrugged her shoulders.

Perri looked up at Evan, who was still pacing around the room. Then she turned back to Tilly. "What happened to all of those people?"

"They stayed. They're out there somewhere." She motioned towards the outside world. "They wanted to explore what our universe was all about. And they've never returned here to try to pass through UnFor again."

Evan stopped pacing and finally spoke up again. "If

the thing sucks in people that want to escape and run away, then why hasn't it just instantly sucked us right back in after we arrived?"

"We did consider that. We believe it is because the curiosity and wonderment is so great that it overpowers the desire to run away. And not to mention the confusion that you must feel in that moment. Having never crossed through myself, I can't relate. I'm just going off what I have observed."

Evan came back to his chair and joined the others. "I guess that seems likely. So, what's the deal with the dome?"

"Well, we thought UnFor was too dangerous for people to accidentally come across. Not because we're afraid people will cross through it. We're confident that no one from our universe would ever want to leave." She wore a smile that made Evan and Perri uneasy. "We wanted to shield the outside world from anyone who enters our universe. We wanted to make sure we were able to evaluate them first before they started roaming around. There's no way of knowing where anyone would come from."

Evan and Perri started to fidget. They were beginning to feel a bit nervous.

Something about what Tilly had just said made them uneasy. Phrases like "shield the outside world" and "evaluate them first" were throwing up red flags in their minds.

"I thought you just studied your light trees? What do

you have to do with evaluating people from parallel universes?" Perri blurted out.

Tilly smiled. "Since we were the first ones to discover UnFor, our group was given free rein on what to do with it. I'm not sure how things work in your universe, but here in our universe, it doesn't matter how important something is deemed. Whoever discovered it first gets to decide what happens."

Evan grabbed Perri by the hand and yanked her up from the chair. Running for the door.

Tilly laughed.

"What on earth are you two doing? You've already been evaluated! Relax. You're free." She was still wearing that smile that made them uneasy.

Evan responded, "What do you mean we've already been evaluated?"

"The metal pathway that you landed on when you got here, the one you walked on the whole way to this building? It scanned your entire system for any potential diseases you might've been carrying, and it performed a full psychoanalysis to ensure that you weren't emotionally unstable or harboring malicious intentions."

"Well, then what's this room for?" Perri asked suspiciously.

"Oh, this is just a place for you to stay. Like a hotel. Except it's free, of course. We provide our visitors with amenities and even some money so that you can stay and explore our universe. If you decide you want to stay, then we can help you get settled in somewhere. But if you decide you want to leave, then all you have to do is come back here and UnFor will take care of the rest." She rose up from the bed and opened up a drawer in the corner of the room.

Perri was starting to relax, but Evan was still a bit hesitant. When Tilly reached down into the drawer, he shielded Perri and said, "What are you doing? Don't try it."

Tilly reached her hand out to Evan and showed that she was holding two of those pens that she had used earlier to imprint the clock on her hand. "Here. Each of you take one of these. This is how you can get back into not only the dome, but also this room when you need to sleep. I'm going to again assume that you do not have this in your universe. It is an imprinter. It will imprint anything you think of into your skin."

"So, it gives us tattoos?" Perri asked.

"That's very primitive. But yes. In a way. Don't think of it as though ink is being embedded into your skin. This is much more advanced. It simply recolors the molecules in your skin. Or at least it tricks your brain and technology into thinking so. And the best part is you can revert it back to normal any time you no longer want the imprint."

They took the imprinters from Tilly. She described for them the symbol they'd need to imprint on their hand in order to unlock the doors. Then she handed them both a tiny metal cube about the size of a standard six-sided die, which she informed them was money. She told them all they needed to do was keep that in their pockets and it would automatically be used at the time of checkout whenever they made purchases. They didn't need to do anything.

"Thank you," Evan said. "For doing this. For helping us and allowing us to explore here. I'm sorry we seemed a bit suspicious of you at first."

She smiled. "I completely understand. And thank you for understanding why we had to evaluate you and look after our people. Now go explore what we have to offer. You just might like it!"

She escorted Perri and Evan out of the room and back through the luminous forest, her silver robes flowing behind her as she guided them. She showed them the exit out of the dome, and they both walked outside.

"Well?" Perri said. "I don't know about you, Pete. But I'm actually a little bit excited to see this universe now. I know I was in shambles a little bit ago, but let's check this place out!"

Evan gave her a nervous smile. He felt his head starting to hurt a little bit, but he didn't want to tell her. Not yet. She was in such a better mood than she was earlier that he didn't want to spoil it. At least not before they explored this place a bit. He knew the pain was going to come, but it could wait.

It wasn't worth wiping that smile off of her face just yet.

CHAPTER TWELVE

When they left the dome, it was quickly apparent to them that this universe was vastly more advanced than their own. Most of what they saw was unrecognizable from the world they left. They knew they were in a parallel equivalent of their home, but they'd never be able to tell had they not already known that fact.

This world was very bright. Very colorful. Lights were everywhere. The trees and plant life illuminated the world, and the buildings were extravagant. They stretched as far as the eye could see. Too many to count. And there were vehicles everywhere. Traditional cars driving on the road, cars flying high above them, even people on bikes that were both grounded and airborne. It was incredible.

There was almost too much to see that they didn't know where to look first. Perri's eyes were full of excitement and wonder. "Evan. This place is just so beautiful. It's no wonder that the other people decided to stay. I mean, I know we haven't been here long or seen much. But just this sight alone. It's so gorgeous."

Evan couldn't stop looking in all directions at all the different people passing them by. No one seemed to notice them. But he was paying attention to everyone he saw. They all looked happy.

He thought maybe they *should* stay. That maybe they could be happy there. "Yeah," he said. "Look at how happy everyone seems. I haven't seen a single person that looks miserable or anything. Everyone looks genuinely happy. Like Tilly said."

"I wonder what it is about this place that makes it like that," Perri said. "It's one thing to just look like a beautiful place. But this is all these people have known. So, there's gotta be more to it than that. Maybe there's just some sort of energy that this universe gives off that makes people innately happy. Sounds weird, but so does a hole in the fabric of reality." She looked at Evan with a smirk.

Evan closed his eyes, trying to focus on blocking out the increasing pain he was feeling in his head.

"You okay?" Perri asked, looking concerned.

"Yeah. Just wondering if maybe we should stay here, Pete. Like all those other people. What if what you said is true? If this place makes people happy, then it's perfect." He winced and then found a nearby bench to sit down on.

Perri followed him and sat down. "Maybe. I just feel like we're giving up pretty quickly on trying to get back home."

"Well, we were planning to run away from there to begin with. And I wanted to stay in the last place we were at, but you suggested we leave."

"That's because of what was going on with our heads, Evan! It was too risky to stay. But so far it doesn't seem like this place is having the same effect on us." She felt her head. No pain. She smiled. "If you really want to stay, then I'm perfectly fine with staying. Let's do it."

Evan fought back the urge to scream due to the pain building up inside his brain. He wasn't sure how much longer he could hold off without telling Perri about it. But he knew she liked it there, and if he mentioned his head she'd make them leave right then.

He smiled and looked at her. "Perfect."

"I have an idea," Perri said. "I think we should use these imprinters to keep a record of how many times we have crossed through The Haze." She took out her imprinter and turned over her wrist, exposing the underside of it. Aiming the imprinter at it, she clicked it. Two black tally marks now appeared on her skin.

"Did that hurt?" Evan asked, looking on in astonishment.

"Nope," Perri answered. "I thought it might. But Tilly was right, these aren't like tattoos. They're something else."

Evan copied what Perri did. He took out his imprinter and clicked it above the same spot on the underside of his wrist. Now two black tally marks were there.

Perri smiled. "And now we'll always remember that it took us two trips to get here. To find this beautiful place."

They got up from the bench and continued to explore the new universe. They walked down the sidewalk until they came to a shop. Once inside, they found all sorts of things they could ever imagine. It had everything. Anything one wanted, that place had it. Literally.

There were standing cubicles that individuals would step inside. Once in, they'd place their feet inside a square on the ground and a beam overhead scanned their brain. Whatever object they thought of, whatever they were in need of, instantly materialized in the cubicle. There were limitations, of course. They couldn't just think of something that was impossible, like a glass of immortality or a planet sized donut. It had to be something that either was feasible or could be manufactured with the current technology.

Naturally, when they each stepped into their individual cubicles, their minds went blank. They had no idea what to think of. They were too excited about the prospects of what could be conjured up. But that didn't stop the machine from doing its thing. After all, the brain is always working, no matter if one realizes it or not. It's always wanting or needing something.

The pain in Evan's head was taking a backseat to the excitement he felt as he stepped inside the square on the ground and felt the beam scan him. He heard a soft, high-pitched chime, and then, to his confusion, a little cube appeared on a table right next to him. He had no idea what it was.

He stepped out of the square and reached down to pick up the cube. It was a little bit bigger than a standard Rubik's Cube, and it seemed to be made of steel. He held it in both hands and examined it. It appeared to have some sort of locking mechanism on the front of it. He shrugged and then walked out of the cubicle to go see what Perri got from hers.

Perri was standing outside of her cubicle clutching a small, thin metal device the size of a stick of gum. She was flipping it over and over in her hands trying to figure out what it was. Then she started tapping on it furiously.

"What the heck are you doing?" Evan asked with a chuckle.

Perri looked up. "Trying to figure out what the heck this thing even is." She held it up to Evan. "What did you get?"

"No idea. This cube thing." He handed her the cube and took her device. After examining the creations their brains thought up, they exchanged items back.

"We'll ask Tilly. I'm sure she can tell us what these things are and what they do," Perri suggested. Then she winced.

"Pete?"

"Oh, Evan," she said. "I just got a really sharp pain in my head." Her eyes widened. She looked terrified. "This must be what you experienced yesterday in the other universe. I don't remember the pain since I had it in my sleep. No. No, no, no. I thought we were gonna be safe here."

Evan knew he was going to need to come clean with her. "Perri. It has already been happening to me."

She stared at him, tears filling her eyes from the pain increasing in her head. "What? Why didn't you say anything?"

"I didn't want to spoil our experience of seeing this place. And you seemed to be having such a good time. I just wanted to stay here, Pete."

She shook her head. "We need to get back to the dome. We need to talk to Tilly."

They looked around for employees so that they could pay for their items. Then they remembered what Tilly said about the payment process. So, they made their way back to the front of the store. As they left the building, they heard a "ding" come from their pockets. It was the little die-shaped payment device processing their payment. And to their surprise, gift bags materialized around their items simultaneously.

They headed back towards the dome to see if Tilly could make any sense as to what was going on with their heads. She seemed to have some knowledge of their pain since she had asked them about it when they first arrived.

"Pete," Perri said, clutching her gift bag with one hand and her head with the other. "I think I just lost something."

"What do you mean?" Evan asked.

"My head. My memory. I think something is gone. I can feel that feeling again. Like something is missing that is supposed to be there."

"Mine is still hurting pretty badly," Evan said. "I don't feel like I've lost anything yet. Aside from this brother you said that I have. What about your parents? Still think they're alive?"

Perri nodded. "Yes. I still don't remember them being dead. Which is weird because I remember being raised at the orphanage with you and everything. And I remember the orphanage closing down and being really upset about that."

Evan stopped in his tracks.

"What?"

Evan looked at Perri nervously. Then he began breathing rapidly and uncontrollably.

"Pete. No, no, no. You need to calm down," Perri said. "What is it? Was it something I said? Or did you lose something now?"

"I know what you lost, Perri." Evan steadied his breathing. "You said the orphanage closed down. But it didn't close down. You've forgotten that it is still around."

"What? No. Evan, this one is you. You're forgetting now. The orphanage closed down. I'm sure of it," Perri said.

Evan was silent as he was thinking about the possibility that she was right. Then he shook his head. "No, Pete. I'm sorry. But I can feel it. The orphanage is still there. You're wrong. The Haze is messing with us."

Perri was getting angry. "Evan. I remember specifically how the loss of that orphanage affected me. And I remember how it affected you, too. That had a big impact on us. I can still feel those feelings. How could I feel those things if it wasn't true?"

"I don't want to fight with you, Pete," Evan said, rubbing his head. "Not again. One big fight is enough for us. I don't want this to escalate to another one. With our emotions high and the pain we're going through, I feel it might. Let's not do that. Not here. Not now. Please. One was enough."

"What are you talking about?" Perri asked. "When

have *we* ever had a big fight?"

Evan smirked at Perri, thinking she was just trying to lighten the tension. Seeing that she wasn't laughing or smiling, his gaze dropped to the ground.

"If what you're saying about the orphanage is true, then that means I'm the one that lost that memory. But you've lost an important one as well. Because we had a really big fight, Pete. The night before we graduated college. It was a whopper."

Perri was silent, staring back at Evan. After a few minutes of the silence, she simply choked out, "We need to get back to Tilly."

CHAPTER THIRTEEN

When they finally reached the dome, Evan pulled out his imprinter and followed Tilly's instructions. He clicked it, and the symbol of Tilly's organization appeared on the back of his hand. He held it up to the door, and it slid open.

Once inside the dome, they saw a few other silver-robed individuals working. They turned out to be some of Tilly's fellow dendroluminologists. Perri and Evan went up to one and asked where Tilly was. Once they were pointed in her direction, they followed the path until they reached her.

"Done exploring so soon?" Tilly said, as she heard them come up next to her. When she looked at them and saw the pained expressions on their faces, she said, "It's happening, isn't it?"

They both nodded.

Tilly took them back to the building that was earlier revealed to be their temporary housing. She encouraged them to lie down on the beds, and she took a seat in one of the chairs in the room. She asked for them to explain when the pain started and how severe it was. They mentioned that Evan's started shortly after leaving the dome, and Perri's started when they were in the shop.

Tilly raised her eyebrows upon hearing they'd visited

one of the shops already. She asked to see what they'd procured. They told her they had no idea what their items were.

She looked at Evan's cube first. "Ahhhh," Tilly said, examining the cube. "This is an encrypted memo-box. You simply record whatever you want on the inside, and then you set a four-letter or number combination as the lock. When it is unlocked and opened, the recorded message is revealed." She smiled. "These are fun. I haven't seen one in ages. People don't use them much anymore. They're a bit outdated."

She placed the memo-box back inside the bag and set it next to Evan's bed. When she took Perri's small metal device out of her gift bag, she let out a gasp that made everyone jump.

"This is…remarkable!" she said. "It's no wonder you thought of this. Genius, really. Granted, we only use these to keep track of rogue clones. But I suppose it should still work the same. Only one way to find out."

Perri chimed in. "What are you talking about, Tilly? Rogue clones? I didn't just think of whatever that is on my own. It just happened. So, what is it?"

"Fascinating," Tilly said, studying Perri's face. "This is a DNA tracker. Like I said, it's meant for tracking down pesky clones that aren't doing what they should be. The user holds their thumb on this little metal dot to the left of the center. Then the coordinates of all clones with 100% identically matching DNA appear on the right."

Evan shot up out of the bed. "So, we could use that

thing to see if we have doppelgangers in this universe!"

Tilly snapped her fingers. "Precisely."

"If it simply tracks DNA, what's to stop it from just displaying the coordinates of a strand of hair on the ground? Or a fingernail?" Perri asked.

Tilly's eyes lit up. "That's a fantastic question, Perri! Simply put, that sort of tracking wouldn't yield the tightest results. So, our devices are of the utmost quality and scale. They track the entire unit. That is to say, an entire body."

"What if they're dead?" Evan chimed in.

"I beg your pardon?" Tilly asked.

"Does it still track them if they're dead?"

A grim expression washed over Tilly's face. "Well, yes. Most unfortunate. But this is something we needed to know. We have to keep track of all clones. Alive or dead. So, yes…. Unfortunately, when you reach the coordinates listed, it is quite possible that you could find yourselves with the unpleasant surprise of having been lead to a deceased individual. I'm sorry."

Perri clutched her head and screamed. The pain was so severe it made her pass out.

Evan looked at Tilly. "You've seen this before. The other visitors before us."

"Yes. And it will pass. Your friend will be fine. She just needs to rest. As do you. I will come back and check on you tomorrow."

Evan nodded and thanked Tilly. She left the room and Evan looked over at Perri. Nervous about all that was happening to them.

He still had no idea what was causing everything. It didn't make any sense. He decided that they would try to figure it all out after they had rested and the pain had passed.

When morning came, Evan and Perri were awakened by the sound of Tilly bringing them food to eat. They were surprised to see that they had actual legitimate food. They figured that with this universe being so technologically advanced, they wouldn't have real food anymore. That they would just take a pill and not have to eat for days. Tilly laughed at that thought and said it was preposterous.

After they had finished eating their breakfast, they told Tilly that they were feeling much better. Then they explained to her the memory loss they experienced.

She informed them that the previous visitors had also gone through bouts of memory loss when they first arrived. Evan asked her if she or her team had any idea what caused the losses. Tilly explained that they were still unclear. She said it was apparent that there was a connection between the memory loss and the headaches, but that's it.

"Maybe it's affecting us because we can't exist in the same universe as our counterparts?" Evan suggested.

Tilly thought about that, but then Perri chimed in. "Evan, that can't be true. Because I didn't have a counterpart in that other universe, remember? And I still experienced a loss."

She took the DNA tracker and placed her thumb on the metal dot. It chimed a dull tone and then the word

"None" appeared on the right side of the device.

"Looks like I have no counterpart here, either," Perri said. She tossed the device to Evan. "You try." Evan did the same thing, and he got the same result as Perri. No counterpart.

"How many times have you crossed over exactly?" Tilly asked.

"Twice," Evan answered. "The second time brought us here."

"So, you've been away from your home, your universe, for a bit now?"

Perri looked at Evan and then back at Tilly. "It's been a couple of days. It was nearly nightfall when we accidentally crossed the first time. And we spent the night in that universe. Then we crossed over to this one the next day. Which was yesterday. But I'm not sure how time is affected between all these universes. To us it's only been a couple of days."

"It's quite possible," Tilly said, "that the longer you're away from your home universe, the worse things are going to get for you. The more memories you could lose."

Perri and Evan exchanged looks of worry.

"But I could be wrong. Like I said, the previous visitors never came back once they decided to stay. If my theory is correct, then they have probably lost all of their memories by now. But if I'm wrong, then they're out there just fine and we're no closer to figuring out your case."

"So, we have two options," Evan said grimly. "We

stay here, away from our universe, and risk losing our memories completely. Or we leave this place to try to get home, which we have no idea how to do, and could still potentially lose our memories completely."

Tilly nodded, a solemn expression on her face. "We do have a theory for how you might be able to get home. Though again, no one has ever tried to go back to their universe. But we have considered the possibilities for each of our visitors in case they chose that route."

Perri spoke up. "You sure have a lot of theories and don't seem to have solid information."

Tilly snorted. "Well, how could we, child? UnFor is an unexplainable, natural phenomenon that won't work for us. We are merely observers of it. And even so, this isn't an absolute science. We are dealing with something beyond our comprehension, our understanding."

"You're right," Perri said. "I'm sorry. I shouldn't have been rude. I'm just stressed."

Evan looked at Perri. Then he directed his voice at Tilly. "What's your theory on how we can get home?"

Perri looked at Evan, eyebrows raised. "You want to go home?"

"No, I don't WANT to go home, Pete. But we need to at least try, right? If what Tilly says is correct and the longer we're away, the worse we'll get, then we need to get back to our universe. We need to try whatever we can."

Perri nodded. "You've grown so much, Pete. You aren't freaking out. You aren't being negative. Look at you. You're stealing my thunder."

Evan smirked.

Tilly smiled and waited patiently until they were finished with their moment.

When it was silent, she answered Evan's question. "My theory is in regards to UnFor's apparent mystical ability to read your thoughts and feelings." She could tell by the looks on their faces that they weren't following her. "It seems to only draw in those who have the feelings and intentions of running away. So, maybe if you can somehow channel your thoughts and feelings to your specific home, your specific universe, at the time you pass through it, it'll take you where you want to go."

"That's genius!" Perri said. "Evan, still want to try it?"

"Yeah. We need to get home," he said.

Perri slipped her DNA tracker into her pocket with her imprinter and gave the die-shaped currency cube back to Tilly. Evan returned his currency cube as well.

"I have something for you," Tilly said. "A parting gift. It's not much, but it's practical." She handed Perri a leather backpack. "Everyone on a journey needs a backpack. This is the nicest we have. Besides, you don't want to carry around that gift bag all day. Put your items in here to keep them safe, and if you stumble into any other universes, then this will come in handy. And if you make it back home, then this bag can simply serve as a reminder of me and our world." Tilly beamed at them.

Perri handed the backpack to Evan since she was already using her own pockets for her items. He tucked his memo-box safely away inside the bag along with his imprinter. And then they followed Tilly out of the building and back out into the dome. Since they now had the intention of leaving again, they didn't want to get too close to The Haze just yet, as it would start drawing them in. They wanted to make sure they had everything ready first.

They thanked Tilly for everything she had done for them. She told them to be careful. And reminded them that her theory might not work and not to be upset. But to keep trying. They smiled and took in their surroundings one last time. One last look at the beautiful luminous trees in the glass dome.

Then Perri and Evan looked at each other, held hands, and began running towards The Haze. They closed their eyes when they felt their feet start moving on their own towards it. They had one thing on their mind.

Home.

Their home.

Their universe.

The good stuff and the bad. Everything that made home, home. The orphanage. The Company. All that had led them to where they were now. They were ready to go back. They needed to be home.

They felt their skin burning and freezing at the same time, then a surge of electricity course through their bodies.

They opened their eyes and then they heard the screams.

CHAPTER FOURTEEN

Evan and Perri opened their eyes, and what they saw filled them with horror. The sky above them was littered with what appeared to be a mixture of dark gray clouds and smoke. The air around them was thick, and they found it difficult to breathe. The scent of something akin to burning rubber engulfed them. They covered their noses and mouths with the collars of their shirts.

It was evident that Tilly's theory on them returning home turned out to be incorrect. This was not their universe. It couldn't have been.

What should've been a lush green forest with a small hidden river running through it, was a wide open wasteland. There were large plumes of smoke billowing skyward some distance away. The screams they heard as they emerged from The Haze continued to sound, apparently coming from the direction of the smoke.

Perri reached into her pocket and pulled out the imprinter. She turned her wrist over and held the device above her exposed flesh. Clicking it, another tally mark appeared. Now showing a total of three marks on the underside of her wrist. "Mark your wrist, Pete. This clearly isn't home. Tilly was wrong. It didn't work. We don't know how many times we're going to do this or how much we're going to forget. Best to keep track."

Evan pulled his imprinter out of the backpack and marked his wrist as well. "But what's the point in even doing this?"

Perri shrugged. "I don't know. Maybe it'll help us to remember if we forget. I'm out of ideas here, Pete. At this point maybe anything is better than nothing. Maybe just establishing a routine or habit will help."

Evan scoffed. They were both frustrated and upset. Not with each other but at the fact that they still weren't home. And they were no closer to figuring out what was happening to them and their memories.

Just then, they heard the sounds of the screams again, this time followed by an explosion. When they looked in the direction of the smoke plumes, they saw a ball of fire and then a new plume arise. From there, they saw something small in the sky whiz off from the apparent battlezone.

Filled with a mixture of fear, dread, and adrenaline, Evan and Perri started towards the smoke plumes to investigate the source of the screams.

After a few seconds, they both collapsed onto the ground.

"Pete. My head," Evan whispered through gritted teeth.

"I know, Evan. Mine too. This is even worse than before."

"Perri. It feels like I'm gonna die. I don't know what dying feels like. But it's gotta be something like this. My brain feels like it's in a big knot. I can't stand it."

Perri gripped her head with both hands, eyes

squeezed shut. Trying to focus on pushing out the pain. "Just breathe. Take a deep breath. It's gonna be okay, Evan. Everything's gonna be al–"

Another explosion.

That one nearly hit the two of them. It came from overhead and it hit the ground just behind them. The force was so strong that it blasted them into the air and launched them several feet forward.

Evan was knocked out cold. Perri was barely hanging onto consciousness. She had landed on her back, and when she opened her eyes, she learned that the small thing they saw whizzing about near the plumes just moments ago was actually not a small thing. It was a very large craft.

She lifted her head up to look in the direction of where the explosion happened that had almost killed her and Evan. She saw The Haze, but the ground it hovered above was no longer there. Just a massive hole in the earth.

Her eyes rolled up in the back of her head as she faded out of consciousness and passed out.

* * *

After what seemed like days, Perri felt herself being shaken back to reality by Evan. He was leaned over her, cuts all over his face. "Pete. Pete, are you okay? I was knocked out and only just woke up. I don't know how long we've been out. We need to get up and move. Do you think you can?"

Perri took a second to check the feeling in her arms and legs before attempting to stand. She felt as though she had been run over by a tank, but she managed to get up off the ground.

Still shaken by what had happened, she looked around, examining the aftermath of the explosion. She turned around to get a better look at the hole that now appeared underneath The Haze.

"What the heck attacked us?" Evan asked.

"I saw it," Perri said quietly. "Just before I passed out. It was big, Pete. A massive ship in the sky. Unlike anything I've ever seen before."

Evan looked up to the sky and all around. Then his eyes met the massive crater where they once stood. "How in the world are we going to cross through The Haze now? We can't even reach it!"

Perri shook her head. "I have no idea. But we need to keep going to find whoever is out there. Someone else might be hurt and need help. We need to find out what's happening here."

"Well, we gotta move quickly before that thing comes back and decides to blast us again."

They headed off in the direction of the smoke plumes that still shot high into the sky. Now in more of a sprint. There was a lot of ground to cover, as it appeared that whatever had been hit to cause so much smoke was still a long distance away.

After running as far as they could, they collapsed behind a group of large rocks to take rest. Between the massive headaches from The Haze, the explosion that knocked them out, and the long-distance sprinting, Evan and Perri wondered if they'd even be able to get back up and continue.

"Hey, Pete?" Evan looked over at Perri who was still trying to catch her breath. She looked up at him in acknowledgment. "I never told you why I was late coming over that day."

Perri looked at Evan, puzzled. Her eyebrows were raised, waiting for him to elaborate.

"The day you got in your bad car accident," he continued. "I never told you why I was late that day. See, it was my fault that you got in that accident. You know me, I'm never late to things. I love plans. Well, my plans had changed that day and I wanted to surprise you. And of course you, being you, got worried since I was late, and you went looking for me. Wrong place, wrong time. Got in your wreck."

Evan was fumbling through his words. Getting more nervous as he spoke. Trying to piece together everything he was going to say. Perri just kept looking at him. Also feeling nervous at what he was getting at. She waited in anticipation for him to finish what he was trying to say.

"I wanted to come clean to you. You see, I rode in the ambulance with you on the way to the hospital. You were out cold, so I know you don't remember that. But even during your recovery at the hospital, every single day, I was there. I wrestled with the notion of finally coming clean and telling you. But I didn't. And then things sort of fell back to our normal rhythm once you got out of the hospital and back home. So, I never said anything. But now. I don't know why now. But it just feels right. I mean, good God, Pete, we almost just died. Literally. Almost just got blown up. I just. I'm sorry, Pete. It's my fault for the wreck. But you deserve to know why it all happened."

Before Evan could continue, he noticed Perri had tears in her eyes, and she looked down at the ground. Then back in the direction of The Haze. Then she started sobbing.

Evan looked petrified. "Wh-what is it? You already knew, didn't you?"

Perri shook her head. "I have no idea, actually. No idea what you're talking about. None of it. I don't remember having a bad car wreck. I don't remember recovering at the hospital. Evan, I don't even have the slightest clue what our 'normal rhythm' is."

She stood up, wiping her eyes. Evan balled his hands into fists and punched the dirt. He yelled out as loudly as he could. It startled Perri. She jumped and turned around to look at him. He had tears rolling down his cheeks.

"I don't understand," he said. "We're losing it all. All the important stuff is slipping away and there's nothing we can do about it! It's not fair."

"I don't think it has anything to do with how long we're away from home, Pete," Perri said. "Think about it. When does this happen to us? Shortly after crossing into The Haze. How many times has this happened to us?"

Evan thought about it for a minute. "Three times, I

think?"

Perri nodded and then turned her wrist over. Displaying the three tally marks that were imprinted in her flesh. "And we have crossed through three times."

Evans eyes widened and he stood up. "It's tied to when we cross through it."

"That's what I'm thinking. That's what makes sense. I'm surprised we didn't figure it out before. But think about it. If we were affected based on how long we were away from home, don't you think we'd have been affected more than just three times by now? It just seems too coincidental that it matches the number of times we've crossed through. And we experience the headaches relatively close together. Or in this last case, at the same time."

"Okay. So, there's one potential mystery solved. But it still poses a big problem. We don't know how to get back home. And the more times we cross, the more memories we're going to lose."

Perri smiled. "But that's the thing, Pete. If this only affects us each time we cross and not by how long we spend away from home, then we may not have to cross through it again. We don't need to get back home."

That made Evan smile, though he still appeared a bit nervous. "You sure you want to take that risk and give up on going home?"

"Well, Tilly said not to give up. But this isn't giving up. This is just us coming up with a theory better than hers. And quite frankly, I think we're right. Besides, as long as we're in this together, there's no risk I wouldn't take." She gave him a wink.

"Who's Tilly?" Evan asked.

The screams sounded again.

CHAPTER FIFTEEN

Perri didn't have time to process the sudden realization of the memory that Evan had lost. There was no time. They had heard the screams several times since entering this universe. They couldn't stall any longer. It was time to see what was going on.

They immediately continued their sprint in the direction of the sound. After a short while, they finally arrived at what they could only guess was the correct place.

It appeared to be some sort of small settlement. There were three large heaps of flaming rubble. It seemed these used to be sheds or buildings of some sort. They were the source of the smoke plumes being sent into the sky that Evan and Perri saw from afar. Nearby, there was a hatch in the ground with a very small window on it.

"Do you suppose the screams came from here?" Evan asked, looking around at the destruction.

Perri walked carefully near the burning structures. She peered around the pile of ash and debris, looking for survivors. "It seemed like it. But I don't see anyone. With all this chaos, you'd think there would at least be bodies if people got hurt."

"Hello?" Evan called out. "Is anyone hurt? Does anybody need help?" He knew there wouldn't be much he could do, but he had to ask. Perri continued to search through the debris but came up short. She was baffled by the lack of people.

"The thing that attacked us is probably the same thing that caused all of this," Perri said. "I just can't figure out where everyone is. We heard people screaming. Loudly. From all the way where we were. They should be here. Or at least what's left of them."

They heard a metal clang behind them. "You clearly don't know what we're dealing with, then. Who are you?"

Evan and Perri turned and saw a tall scruffy man who looked to be in his 40s. He was followed by a woman and a little girl. They were standing near the hatch, which they had clearly just come up out of.

He eyed Evan and Perri closely for several minutes and then began to slowly walk towards them. The woman kept the child close to her as they stayed back at the hatch, remaining close to the bunker evidently hidden below ground.

Evan looked at Perri and then at the man. He was about to speak, but Perri beat him to it.

"My name is Perri Pearson. And this is Evan Miles. It would take too long to explain the details about who we are, but that clearly doesn't seem important." She looked around. "What's going on here?"

The man studied her face. Then he looked back at the woman and child. He walked over to one of the nearby burning structures and then turned to look back at Perri. "It does matter who you are. But I'll fill you in on what's going on because I can tell by the looks on both your faces that you genuinely have no idea. I've seen that look before. But when I'm done, you're telling me who you are and where you came from."

Perri looked back at Evan who gave her a nod. Then she simply said, "Okay."

"My name is James. This is my wife and daughter. That's all you need to know about them. I'm sorry, but I don't know you and I don't trust you. We're at war."

James cleared his throat. "About six months ago, our planet was invaded. We thought we were making peace with our neighbors out there, but we thought wrong. Out of nowhere, the attacks came. Small at first. So small that we didn't realize what they truly were. Small. Heh. They weren't small then. But on a global, grand scale like today, they're small. Things here and there that were mistaken for terrorist attacks. We turned on each other. Ever since the peace treaties, we haven't known war for decades." James started pacing back and forth from each of the burning structures.

"When these attacks started, everyone was confused. But the fingers had to be pointed somewhere. Rather than pointing them at the sky, we pointed them at each other. First couple of months' worth of casualties were from ourselves. Self-inflicted. Then the attacks got bigger, more sophisticated. That's when we started opening our eyes to what was right in front of us. Or above us, rather. Their technology allowed them to sneak the smaller attacks in without us noticing them. But in order for them to do the bigger ones, they couldn't go undetected. But at that point, I don't think they cared anymore. We had done some of their work for them by taking each other out.

"They made it known to us that they were taking this planet. They had no interest in us, so they were set on wiping our species out entirely. No attempt at peace was successful. That's how bad it was. They were not going to stop until we were all gone. We wiped about a quarter of our own human population out ourselves before they even made themselves known. Before we even knew who the real enemy was. But by then it was too late. We didn't stand a chance. They obliterated us before we even had time to figure out their true nature and their weaknesses. Before we had time to mount a worthy defense. There is no counterattack. There is no defeating them. Survival is all that's left."

Perri and Evan were stunned.

They had never imagined an actual alien invasion could happen. Not in real life. Even though they'd been crossing over into parallel worlds, the thought never crossed their minds. Similar realities, technologically advanced realities–but a reality devastated by an extraterrestrial race?

It was way worse than they'd imagined.

James walked over to his family. He kissed his daughter on the top of the head and squeezed his wife's hand as he paced by them and back over towards where Perri and Evan stood in shock.

"It's hard to say exactly, but by now I'd wager there's

probably only about a tenth of the human species left. And that's being generous, honestly. If they sent more of their fleet here we'd have probably been wiped out in a day. But that's what makes them more terrifying. They're patient. They know they don't need to wipe us all out instantly. Because they know they're going to get us in the end. They're the slow killers. That's why there are only a few ships circling the globe. They search for any stragglers and then they eradicate them."

James finally stopped speaking. He walked back over to the rubble that was still burning. Watching as the smoke continued to billow up into the sky, he crossed his arms and shook his head.

Perri, still reeling from the information that was just provided, spoke up. "We…we heard screams. Loud screams."

"The reason you see no bodies is because their blasts obliterate us." James turned around so that he was staring Perri directly in the eyes. "Literally. Completely obliterates us. When it hits human flesh it completely disintegrates us on a molecular level."

James' wife and daughter began to let out some soft cries. Evan looked over at them and then back at James, who was now staring at them with a sullen expression on his face. After sweeping his eyes over the crumbled structures one more time, Evan said, "There were more of you."

James nodded.

Evan closed his eyes and lowered his head. "I'm so sorry."

"As am I," Perri said, a catch in her voice. "This is truly horrifying."

"We were a small community out here. We've been here for about two months. Stumbled across this old abandoned lot while escaping what was left of the city. There were two other families. We were close. We built a bond with them. We were all just trying to survive together. We used these buildings here as part of our little community. School for the kids, quarantine area when we got sick, and then a place for our animals. That bunker underground is where we all stayed. It's quite large and roomy under there. Plenty for us all.

"We thought we would be safe. We haven't seen any activity, no ships, nothing in this area the whole time we've been here. Until this morning. See, we always rotated chores as families. One of the families was above ground taking care of the animals when the first attack came. They didn't see it coming. It must have taken out the animal building, just missing them. We felt the explosion underground and we heard them scream. The other family went up to check. Before they went above, we heard another scream and felt another explosion. Then it was silent. We waited for a few minutes, but then the other family darted out to check. I tried to get them to wait longer but they wouldn't listen."

James kicked a nearby piece of rubble and muttered a curse to himself. "We heard them scream and then felt another explosion." His voice was shaking now. "I grabbed my family and held them as tightly as I could. And we stayed huddled under the ground. It was silent for a few minutes, and then we felt a very faint explosion, like it came from a distance away. So, we thought they were leaving." Tears welled up in his eyes. "After a few hours of sitting in silence and praying that it was over, I finally opened up the hatch and looked at the horror that you now see before you. Our community destroyed. Our friends gone.

"And. I thought it was safe. I thought we were in the clear. I motioned for my wife and daughter to come out. No sooner had they come out of that hole in the ground did we hear the sound of that dreaded ship in the sky above us. They screamed and I shouted for them to dive back underground, then I found a speed I'd never found in my life. By some miracle, we made it back under there safely. But I nearly got us killed." James wiped the tears away from his face and joined his family.

Perri grabbed Evan's hand. "Keeping family safe is the most important thing. Family is the most important thing."

"Now you know everything that's been going on. It's your turn to spill. Like I said. I could tell from your faces that you had no idea what was going on. Only time I've seen those looks was when this thing was just beginning. So, you better get to talking."

Perri and Evan exchanged looks. Then Perri walked towards James. "You probably won't believe what we have to say. But I ask you to keep an open mind. We come from a different universe and we got here by mistake."

James' daughter looked up at her mom, who in turn

looked over at her husband who had his eyes narrowed, contemplating what he just heard.

"Have you looked around? Our world is on the brink of total annihilation by a species from outer space. You have my undivided attention," James said calmly.

Perri and Evan took turns explaining to them what had happened thus far. They explained all about The Haze and how they'd accidentally stumbled through it, then how they'd been trying to get home. Unsuccessfully, of course. They explained that they always experienced a severe headache after passing through it, and that passing through was also accompanied by some sort of memory loss that appeared to be permanent.

They then showed them the few gadgets they brought with them from the previous universe. The imprinters, Evan's memo-box, and Perri's DNA tracker. That prompted Perri to use the tracker to see if they had doppelgangers there. Nope. It appeared they either didn't exist in this universe or had already been obliterated completely, as there would be no bodies for the tracker to even locate.

"Well, this really is pretty wild," James said, sounding truly surprised. "No wonder you two had no idea what you stumbled into. I can imagine this must be quite the shock."

"You know," Evan said, "why don't you come with us?"

Perri turned to him, eyes wide. "Evan! That's a great idea!" Then she turned back to James. "The Haze isn't really that far from here. It's crazy how close you guys have been to it this whole time, really. We can travel there and you guys can leave this place!"

James thought about it. Then he said, "I thought you said there's no way to control where you end up?"

"Well, yeah, that's true," Perri stammered.

"Then how do we know we wouldn't just end up somewhere even worse?"

Evan butted in. "That's up to you to decide if that's a risk you'd be willing to take. This is your world, not ours. But from what we've seen so far, this doesn't seem like a place worth being in. Seems pretty much doomed. Wouldn't you rather risk it, if there's a chance of ending up in a much safer, nicer place?"

James looked at his family. "These headaches. Really bad, huh?"

"I won't lie to you. They're not great. But they do pass," Perri said.

"And it makes you lose your memory, too?"

Evan nodded. "Yes. We don't really have any solid answers for you there. We're still having trouble with that one. But from what we've gathered, that seems to be tied to the headaches, which seem to be tied to when you cross into The Haze itself. So, if you only cross once and end up in a great place…just endure one headache and pray you don't lose a precious memory. But again, it's a risk you have to decide if it's worth taking."

"We need to think about it for a bit. Is that okay? Are you in a hurry to leave?"

Perri shook her head. "No, please do think about it. This is going to change your life. It is most certainly a risk, but we will help you. I think maybe we were sent to this universe to help you." She smiled at him.

James and his family invited Evan and Perri down into the bunker to rest and to have something to eat while they thought about their decision.

After a couple of hours pondering what would be the biggest decision of their lives, James and his wife came to a conclusion.

They were going to do it.

They were ready to leave that wasteland of a world in hopes of finding a better one for their daughter. For their family.

Everyone left the bunker and started off back in the direction of The Haze. Once they reached the large group of rocks that Evan and Perri had rested at before, Perri reiterated to James and his family what it would feel like when they got close to The Haze. How it would start to pull them in and how they would feel a sense of calmness when they looked at it. She also told them what they would feel when crossing through.

"How do we make sure we end up at the same place?" James asked.

Perri and Evan exchanged glances. They hadn't actually thought of that because they had always ended up in the same place, which they had assumed was simply due to them crossing at the same time.

"I think the fact of us crossing at the same time ensures we'll end up in the same place. Evan and I have always arrived at the same place."

"You 'think?' No, no, no. 'Think' is not good enough for me. This is my family. My wife and daughter. I'm not going to risk being separated into different universes from them. Are you kidding me?" James was snappy, and irritation grew on his face.

"Well," Evan said, looking over at his friend, "Perri and I have always held hands as we crossed through it. Obviously, it's a guess because there's no way to know for sure. But it seems like maybe as long as you're touching, you'll end up at the same place."

Perri considered that and then looked at James, who was doing the same. He studied Evan and then nodded his head. "Now that sounds plausible." He scrunched up his face, as if thinking deeply about it for a few minutes. "Yes, I suppose it does make sense."

They continued heading in the direction of The Haze when a sudden realization washed over Evan. "Wait a minute. Pete!" He grabbed Perri and turned her to face him. "The Haze. How are we going to reach it? Remember, there's a big humongous hole underneath it now!"

Perri gasped. "I completely forgot. I was too busy focused on getting them here."

"What's the problem?" James asked, eyebrows raised.

They explained to him about the explosion that had almost killed them when they'd first arrived. "So, that was you guys. That was the small blast we felt from inside our bunker. Well, if this Haze thing drags us into it, do you think it'll just drag us right over that hole?"

"Maybe," Perri said, looking concerned. "We'll know soon enough. We're nearly there." She pointed up ahead. They could all just barely see The Haze in the distance.

Just then they heard something whiz across the sky above them. The large alien craft had made its way back around the globe and found them.

"It's here!" James yelled. He picked up his daughter with one hand and grabbed his wife's hand with the other, then they began sprinting towards The Haze. Evan and Perri also grabbed each other's hands and were sprinting closely behind the family.

The ship hovered above for a minute without firing on them. As if it were observing what they were doing. It seemed like the aliens saw The Haze and were curious to see what it did.

When James and his family reached the edge of the massive crater, The Haze began pulling them in towards it, just like he thought it would. They were now hovering in the air over the crater. He let out a very calm "Thank you" before he and his family vanished into The Haze.

When Evan and Perri reached the edge of the crater, The Haze began pulling them in as well. They both felt that sense of calmness wash over them as they were getting closer.

Having seen James and his family disappear through The Haze, the aliens must have decided they couldn't allow it to happen again.

Just as Evan and Perri were about to cross through, an explosion hit right below them and Perri felt Evan's grip on her hand loosen.

Everything felt as though it went in slow motion. She could feel their fingers slowly slide away from each other as the blast pulled them apart.

She turned her head at the last second before crossing through and saw Evan's navy blue eyes staring into hers as he was sent flying backwards away from The Haze, his hand still outstretched for hers.

Perri cried out for him at the top of her lungs, but it was no use. It was over.

She emerged from the other side of The Haze.

Alone.

CHAPTER SIXTEEN

Shock. Fear. Pain. These things flooded Perri. She couldn't believe what had just happened. Evan. Just moments ago his hand was clutching hers. Until she watched as he was thrown back and they were separated. And there was nothing she could do.

Now her hand felt empty.

She dreaded to think what was happening to him at that very moment. What had happened when he was thrown in the blast? Was he dead? Did the blast obliterate him? Did the aliens capture him? Her mind was racing. Her thoughts, her feelings, she couldn't control them. She felt the air escaping her lungs faster than she could take more in. Her chest was tightening and she couldn't breathe. Her mouth was so dry she thought she would die of thirst any second.

She didn't bother to look at her surroundings. Perri ran until she found some water. She cupped her hand down into a nearby stream and brought it to her lips. Then she gasped for breath, trying to steady her breathing. She tried to relax her mind and calm her thoughts, but it did no good. She felt a surge of pain rush through her head and then she collapsed.

* * *

A full day passed until Perri regained consciousness.

When she came to, she realized that she'd better try to find something to eat. But part of her didn't even want to bother. She was too upset to eat. She didn't care that she was hungry. Food was the last thing she wanted at that moment.

All she wanted was Evan.

Thinking of what had happened to him was tearing her up. Driving her crazy. She half wanted to run back towards The Haze, so that it would pull her in. But she also knew it would probably be better to compose herself and try to think clearly before crossing again.

First thing she needed to do was make the mark. She grabbed the imprinter and created the fourth tally mark in her skin on the underside of her wrist. When she stowed it back into her pocket, she pulled out the DNA tracker. After placing her thumb on the metal pad, she was stunned to hear, for the first time since having it, a short, high-pitched melodic trill. After which, a set of coordinates appeared on the right side of the device.

Her eyes widened at the realization that she actually had a doppelganger in this universe. She was unsure of the location just based off a simple set of coordinates, so she knew that venturing into civilization was going to be a must. Perri wondered if she might find a place similar to her home, a place with advanced technology, or a place ravaged by an alien invasion. Judging by the desolate plains she was standing in, it could be anything.

As she made her way into the city, she tried hard not to think about anything at all. Because she knew the more she thought, the more she would only think about Evan. And that wasn't helping. She needed to remain as calm as possible. Being level-headed and calm was who she was. Though she didn't always remain calm. There were times Evan was the calm one. Even just within the past few days as they'd been going through those universes.

Evan.

She really couldn't keep her mind off of Evan. If he was still alive, there was no way he was calm. Perri knew that she helped relax him and helped him when he got overwhelmed by everything. She couldn't imagine how panicked he must be. Especially considering how panicked she actually was.

Feeling her chest start to tighten again, Perri focused her breathing. Then she broke down.

She made it into town and found the nearest bench on the nearest sidewalk, then she collapsed down onto it. She cried.

Why was all of it happening? What had they done so wrong that they deserved to be not only stranded away from home, but also separated from each other? They were the only family they had left. Even though Perri didn't remember her parents' death anymore, it didn't change the fact that they were gone.

Why were they so stupid to run away to begin with? If they'd never had the idea to run, they wouldn't have gone over the plans, which means they wouldn't have come across The Haze. What was so bad that they had been prepared to change their lives? What had even caused them to run away?

She had so many thoughts running through her mind as the tears were streaming down her face. Then she sat up and wiped her eyes and nose. She stared blankly ahead in the distance.

The thought crossed her mind again.

What had caused them to run away?

Perri jumped up off the bench. That must be the next memory that was taken from her. She could feel it. She could feel the gap in her mind where it should have been.

One day they had been just fine, working and hanging out after work like usual. And then the next day, she just remembered going to Evan's house and the two of them going to look at the boat. She remembered everything that took place. Finding the boat, trying to get it back to that little nook, and getting sucked into The Haze. But she couldn't remember why they were running away in the first place.

Whatever the reason, she knew it was no longer worth it. Not by a long shot.

Perri felt as though she was reaching an internal crossroads. Knowing her doppelganger was in this universe somewhere made her want to contact her somehow. But to what end? What would be the point? She knew that this Perri wouldn't be able to help her find Evan. No one could. Not even Tilly.

But something made her feel like she should find her. However, Perri also felt as though she just wanted to find a soft bed, so she could curl up and sleep for days on end. To just put all of it out of her mind. Hoping beyond hope that it was nothing more than a bad dream. That she would just wake up and she'd be back at her home in her universe. Waking up to go to work at The Company.

She looked around and realized the city she was standing in looked somewhat familiar. It actually looked similar to the first universe her and Evan crossed into. Meaning that it bore a striking resemblance to her own universe. Nothing seemed too different about it. At least not yet.

With things looking roughly the same, she knew that finding her way around town should be fairly simple. She strode off in the direction of the library, hoping that it was open. After all, she had absolutely no idea what day it was or the time.

To her relief, it was open and she made her way inside. It was time to enter the coordinates from the DNA tracker into a computer and see where her doppelganger was currently located.

She recognized the location that was brought up on the map, and it intrigued her. It was the orphanage. Or at least where the orphanage was in her universe.

Before leaving the library, Perri decided to browse the computer and see if she could find a record of Evan in this universe. See if there was a counterpart of him. Then she could at least see his face. It wouldn't be her Evan, but it would at least be a version of him. Someone she could talk to. He couldn't be too different.

Her heart raced as she thought of the prospect of

meeting another Evan, just as she had in that first universe.

Simply searching for his name as a resident there yielded no results. She then searched for records of the car accident that had killed his family to see if that incident had ever happened. No records were found. She searched for his parents' names in the city's historical records and found them, but it appeared they had moved away many years ago with their only child. A daughter named Erin.

It seemed that in this universe, Evan didn't exist. His parents had had a daughter instead.

Feeling hopeless, Perri left and sluggishly headed in the direction of where her doppelganger was. Where, according to the coordinates on the DNA tracker, the orphanage from her universe was located. There was no telling what would be in that location in this universe. And she had no idea what to do about her doppelganger.

Was she just going to waltz in and go up to her, looking like she did? That would draw attention. But at that point, she didn't really care. She was prepared to wing it and do whatever came to her mind.

As Perri neared the destination, it appeared that the orphanage did, indeed, exist in this universe. Once again, her sensible side came through and told her that she couldn't go in there in her current state. She figured it wasn't a common occurrence for someone to have an exact duplicate of themself suddenly come into their life and then claim to be from another universe. No, she needed to play it differently. How on earth was she possibly going to disguise herself?

Then it came to her. The imprinter.

Tilly had explained to them that it didn't simply give them tattoos. No, it tricked the brain into thinking that it changed the colors of the molecules in one's skin. Maybe she could try to use it to color her visible skin.

She hid behind a tree, pulled out the imprinter, and got to work coloring every bit of skin that was showing. After several minutes of concentration, the process was complete. She looked herself over and it appeared to have done the trick. Her skin was now a deep blue color, and she even added some extra flourishes in the form of all sorts of various random shapes and tribal-looking marks. Some big, some small. Some white, some black.

Perri figured it would draw attention away from the fact that she was still clearly the identical twin of whomever was inside that orphanage. She wasn't quite sure how to explain why she looked the way she did. But she had a feeling something would come to her in the moment.

She swallowed a big gulp of air, took a deep breath, and knocked on the door to the orphanage.

A familiar face answered the door, as it was one of the same caretakers who had answered the door in the first universe they had gone to. Apparently that person must be a caretaker in all universes.

Regardless, they took one look at Perri and nearly fainted in surprise. Clearly taken aback by her odd appearance. Perri told the caretaker that she was a traveling performer who had been abandoned by her partner and needed a place to stay. Just until she could figure out where to go next. She really felt awful for lying to the caretaker. Especially since she knew the person. Well, their counterpart from her own universe, at least.

The caretaker was very nervous and apprehensive at first but then agreed to let Perri come inside. But it was explained that she would first need to go through the entrance evaluation before she could be given a room. Just like all residents go through.

Perri questioned that, but the caretaker insisted on it. It was explained that anyone wishing to stay at the facility, whether it be for a night or for a permanent stay, such as in the case of children or staff, must go through an evaluation before they can so much as step into the living room. They had an on-site psychologist who administered all evaluations. Perri was really concerned about having to go through an evaluation just in order to stay, but she felt she didn't have much of an option. She needed to get in to speak with her doppelganger. If she didn't happen to pass her evaluation, then she would just have to figure out something else.

Her mind was so scattered. Her feelings and her emotions were all over the place. Her thoughts were far out of control. There was no telling what sort of results the evaluation would yield.

Normally, she would not be concerned. Normally, she would be the one doing the evaluations. After all, she was the one that went to school for that sort of thing. It was her area of expertise. But that felt like a lifetime ago.

So much had happened since then.

The caretakers led her to an empty room with a couch and a chair. They instructed her to lie down on the couch and said the psychologist would be in momentarily to speak with her. The chair was positioned several feet away from the couch.

Perri lay down and stared up at the ceiling for a few minutes. Thinking about what in the world the evaluation would consist of. What sort of questions they might ask her. Especially considering the fact that she wasn't a child coming to stay there permanently.

Then, as it had been doing, her mind began racing. She started thinking of Evan. Wondering what was going on with him. Wondering if he was alive. Her eyes started to water. She closed them and thought of all the events that had led her there.

Before she could get any more thoughts out, she heard the door behind her open and close. Footsteps got closer and then she heard someone sit down in the empty chair in the room.

"Sorry for the wait. I'm Dr. Pearson and I'll be conducting your entrance evaluation."

Perri's eyes shot open. She recognized that voice.

Of course. Her doppelganger was the psychologist. Why wouldn't she be? It made sense.

"Why don't we start with your name. What is it?"

Perri froze. It felt as though an iron hand had just grabbed hold of her throat. She had no idea what she was going to say.

CHAPTER SEVENTEEN

Perri tried to come up with something, but her mind was entirely blank. Not a single thought managed to conjure up a word for her to say.

The doctor cleared her throat. Then she asked the question again. "Could I please get your name?"

And again, nothing.

"Okay then," Dr. Pearson said, scribbling something on her notepad. "Let's try something else. Why don't you tell me why you're here seeking a place to stay?"

Perri couldn't figure out what was wrong with her. Why couldn't she say anything? Was she nervous? Was she just stupid?

She fidgeted, trying not to let her doppelganger see her face. The tension in the room was high and things felt extremely awkward.

Dr. Pearson set her pen and notepad down in her lap with a thud. "Look. I don't know if you realize it or not, but this is an orphanage. You know, this is a home for children with no families. We aren't just going to allow a random stranger to waltz in off the street and stay here without first evaluating them. If you aren't going to comply with our process, then I'm afraid I'll have no choice but to mark you as having failed this evaluation, and you'll need to seek shelter elsewhere."

She was beginning to sound a bit agitated. Her quick loss of patience and slight rise in temper took Perri by surprise. It seemed as though Dr. Pearson and Perri were definitely a bit different.

Perri finally took a few deep breaths before carefully considering what her first few words to her counterpart were going to be. Then she began to speak.

"I got separated from my partner and have no idea where he is. I am lost and far from home. I don't need to stay for long, just until I can figure out what to do. Please." That was all Perri could muster.

Dr. Pearson began scribbling in her notepad at once, then looked back in the direction of the couch Perri was lying on. "What was your act?" she asked.

"Excuse me?" Perri asked, confused.

"You and your partner. The caretakers said you told them you were a traveling performer. With the blue I can see on your skin from here, I was curious what your act was."

Perri thought for a minute, unsure of what to say. She was a terrible liar and felt guilty for even thinking about lying. Having already lied up to that point made her feel disgusted, but the truth didn't seem like a plausible option. She needed to come up with something and she needed to do it quickly, or else the whole thing would have been a waste of time.

"Our act," Perri started, "was that I am an alien and he's a human, and we sing a song about coexisting peacefully." The words had barely left her lips before she realized how dumb that sounded. Had she really just said that? She and Evan never sang, for one thing. And for another, that was the dumbest sounding act she'd ever heard of. Sure, it might explain why her skin was randomly blue, but if her counterpart was half as smart as she was, she wasn't going to buy it.

The doppelganger scribbled a couple of things down in her notepad and then once again slammed her things down, but that time on a table instead of her lap. Sounding even more agitated, she said, "Okay. Get up. Off the couch. Now. Up."

Perri felt her face flush with embarrassment, though it wouldn't show thanks to the deep blue color of her skin. Shaking with nerves at facing her doppelganger, she slowly stood up from the couch and turned to face Dr. Pearson.

Perri noticed that she was still sitting down in her chair. Arms crossed. She recognized the same chocolate brown hair that was on her own head. Though instead of being worn down to her shoulders like Perri's, her counterpart's was pulled back into a tight ponytail.

Dr. Pearson rose up from her chair without saying a word and gradually walked towards where Perri stood. She stopped when she was about two feet in front of her. They were, of course, standing eye-to-eye. Dr. Pearson shared the same emerald green eyes that Perri had, except hers were shielded behind a pair of small rectangular glasses.

Perri was shaking with nerves, but Dr. Pearson was eerily calm despite the obvious fury. She stared directly at Perri, studying her. Perri couldn't maintain eye contact and found herself looking down at the ground.

They stood in silence for a few minutes, but to Perri it felt like hours.

Finally, Dr. Pearson spoke. "You know, this might come to your surprise, but I am not an idiot," she said in a snappy tone. "Did you think that I wouldn't recognize my own voice?"

Perri's eyes widened. "I never thought you were an idiot. The opposite, actually."

"I knew who you were the moment you first spoke. I just wanted to see if you were ever going to tell the truth. And I was curious as to what sort of things you might say instead."

Perri was shocked. How could she possibly know who she was? And why was she so bitter? Perri could feel the sweat on her own forehead from all the nervousness coursing through her.

Dr. Pearson kept her stern gaze on Perri. "I have very little patience for liars. And even less so for people who refuse to speak. But for it to be coming from me is unacceptable."

That finally got under Perri's own skin. "Okay. I don't know what your deal is, but you need to lighten up. You don't know what's going on. There's no possible way that you could. But I don't appreciate the attitude that you have with me right now. I came here looking for help."

"You're right," Dr. Pearson said, raising her eyebrows. "I don't know what is going on. But I do know that you're me. Or at least a version of me. I don't understand it. But I'm not an idiot. And I'm sorry for the attitude. But like I said before, this is an orphanage. We take the safety of the children very seriously here. I won't tolerate uncooperative people. Even if it's someone who looks like me. So, if you want help, then you need to tell me what is going on."

They both sat down on the couch, and Perri began her story.

She told her counterpart everything that had happened. Everything she could remember, at least. From having a best friend named Evan, to running away. She told her about how they had accidentally gotten pulled into The Haze and, thereby, crossing into another universe for the first time. Told her about the headaches, the memory losses. She told her all they had experienced. Ending with how she had wound up there. Being separated from Evan.

Dr. Pearson was soaking everything in and then finally asked Perri a simple question. "But why did you make your skin blue?"

"Oh." Perri felt a little embarrassed. "I was nervous about meeting you, so I tried to hide who I was. This was all I could think of. I didn't know what else to do."

For the first time, Dr. Pearson actually let out a bit of a chuckle. "Turning your skin blue? A traveling performer? That's the best you could do?" She flashed a smile at Perri.

Perri smiled and then her expression went flat again.

"My brain just feels so fried. My emotions are everywhere. And I'm tired. I'm surprised I thought of anything at all, honestly. I really don't even know why I came to you. It just…felt like I needed to."

Dr. Pearson put her hand on Perri's shoulder. "I'm glad you did. This whole thing is really weird, I gotta say. But if I can help in any way to get you back to your friend, then I'll do what I can."

Perri shook her head. "Thanks. But there's nothing you can do. Really, there's not. It's over. I'll never see him again." She looked down as tears began to fill her eyes.

Dr. Pearson stood up. "You shouldn't stay here." Perri wiped her eyes and looked up at her doppelganger with a confused expression. "Why don't you come stay with me? It'll be nice. We can get to know each other better. And you can tell me more about Evan."

Perri nodded and simply said, "Thank you."

"I do have one condition though," said Dr. Pearson, with a serious expression on her face. "You lose the blue skin and the crazy tribal markings." Then a smile crept over her face.

That made Perri give a little smile. She pulled out the imprinter and within a few minutes, she'd returned back to normal. No more deep blue skin. No more black and white markings. Though, she did replace the four tally marks on her wrist indicating the number of times she had crossed into The Haze.

Dr. Pearson could now see the real Perri for the first time. It was all so bizarre to her. A doppelganger from another universe.

They left the orphanage and went to Dr. Pearson's home. She lived alone, so she was excited for the company.

They spent the next several days getting to know each other. Talking about the differences in their childhoods. Perri learned that Dr. Pearson had grown up with her parents. Then Perri explained how she'd grown up in the orphanage. She mentioned that she no longer remembered her parents had died but that it had happened regardless. She never knew them.

Perri took notice of Dr. Pearson's mannerisms during the time she had spent with her. Noticing more and more how she seemed to have little patience and a quick temper. It baffled her to see it. Perri was not one to be quick-tempered.

One evening when they were talking after dinner, Perri asked her counterpart about it. "Have you always been so easily angered?"

"What do you mean?" asked Dr. Pearson.

"Aside from some of the more obvious differences between our histories, I've noticed a big difference in our personalities. That is, you seem to be quick-tempered. I have always considered myself more laid back, and people say I have a lot of patience. I don't see that in you. I don't mean to be blunt, I'm just curious if something happened or if you've just always been that way."

Dr. Pearson sighed. "It's fine. You're not the first person to say that. And I know that about myself. I'd be a bad psychologist if I couldn't even recognize my own issues, especially after people point them out." She went on to explain that she had never had any friends growing up. Her parents had been strict with her and had never let her do anything with anyone. They had always wanted her to focus on schoolwork and that was it. All she had were her parents and school. So, her social life was practically nonexistent. And it just continued to get worse the older she got. But she found that she was good at analyzing the issues in others, since she'd spent so much of her time observing, never being able to be a part of anything.

"You see, you had Evan. I had no one. If I'd had my own Evan growing up, then maybe I'd have turned out differently. Maybe I'd be more like you. But I didn't have anyone to balance me out. All of my emotions stayed bottled up. Positive and negative. Some days one would win over the other."

Perri looked at Dr. Pearson and felt incredibly sad. She felt like she was looking at what her life would have been like without Evan.

Is that what her life was going to turn into now that he was no longer there? She had grown up with Evan being the negative one of the two of them, so Perri had been forced to be the positive one. Her positive side had always taken hold because it had to. But now that Evan wasn't around to be the negative one, those emotions were bound to come out.

Then, she realized they already had been. She'd been nervous, depressed, anxious, worried—all kinds of things since arriving there. Since losing Evan. Really, she'd been all kinds of everything since The Haze started taking her memories away. Was she starting to forget who she really was?

Dr. Pearson could tell Perri was deep in thought because she had been quiet for some time, and she was up pacing back and forth. Something Dr. Pearson herself was used to doing when she was deep in thought. "What's on your mind, Perri?"

"I'm sorry, but I don't want to end up like you. I don't want to be angry. I don't want to be without him. I need him. And he needs me. It's like you said. Balance. We balanced each other out. I don't know how, but I have to find him."

Dr. Pearson smiled. "Now that sounds like you. That sounds like me. At least I'd like to think it does. You shouldn't give up. You said you felt like you needed to come to me. To see me. There's gotta be a reason. Maybe this is it. Maybe you needed me to spark you back to reality. To make you realize you need to get back out there and search for him. Do you think he's still alive?"

Perri stopped pacing and stared directly at Dr. Pearson. "Yes. He HAS to be. I refuse to believe that he's dead. He's alive. I know it. I believe it. He's out there. My Evan. Pete."

"Then what are you doing here with me? Go find him! Go! I'll head that way with you, but I'm not leaving my universe. I don't want anything to do with that Haze nonsense."

They immediately left Dr. Pearson's house.

Even though it was nighttime, they drove to the

plains where Perri had arrived, left the car parked, and then ran in the direction of The Haze. When they got close, Perri pointed and said, "It's right down there."

"Well, I'm not going any closer then. I don't want to risk getting pulled in. No way. I like my memories. I don't want to lose them like you have." Dr. Pearson gave her a nervous glance.

"Thank you. For everything. Thank you for believing me. For listening to me. For letting me stay with you and talking to me. But above all else, thank you for giving me that spark to keep going. I'm going to find him, I just know it." Perri smiled and gave her doppelganger a hug.

"You're welcome, kid," Dr. Pearson smiled. "I believe in you. I know you'll find him, too. Just don't give up. Remember who you are. Don't ever give up."

"Goodbye, Perri."

"See you later, Perri."

Dr. Pearson watched as Perri ran down towards The Haze.

Perri felt herself getting pulled towards it. She closed her eyes as tightly as she could, and she thought of Evan. His dark orange, untidy hair. Those navy blue eyes of his, staring into hers as they were being separated just a week ago.

Then she crossed into The Haze, feeling her skin burn and freeze.

What she felt next made her eyes jolt open immediately.

She was no longer standing on solid ground—she was in water. A river.

CHAPTER EIGHTEEN

Perri whipped her head around as fast as she could to look at her surroundings. She didn't care that she was standing waist deep in a river. The feeling was so familiar. So welcoming. Her heart was racing. Not only was she standing in a river, but that river was in the middle of a forest.

She ran. Away from The Haze. In a familiar direction.

As she was running, she took her imprinter out and marked her skin. A dark slash appeared through the four tally marks, now making a fifth.

Was she finally home?

When she reached the spot she was running towards, she clambered out of the water and onto the ground. Just yards away from what appeared to be a small little nook at the edge of the forest. She didn't care about the searing pain that was increasing in her head. She didn't care that she was about to pass out. She didn't care what memory that trip through The Haze had cost her. All she cared about was that it felt like she had finally made it back home. To her universe. And now she needed to see if Evan was there, too. Because for the first time since the whole mess started, things finally seemed to be looking up.

All of that talk of running away seemed like ages ago. And for what? To lose memories and to be separated from each other? Only to wind up back home? What a waste.

The pain in her head was becoming so severe she could hardly stand up any longer. Perri nestled herself down on a cool patch of grass just inside the nook to rest until the pain subsided. As she could feel her consciousness slipping away, knowing she was moments from passing out, she thought of the last time she was in the nook when she and Evan discovered the boat had been moved. They had only found the tarp.

She looked around and noticed the tarp wasn't there now. Perri wondered where it was and wished it was there so she could cover up with it. All the shade in the nook actually made it quite chilly. She blinked a few times and then she faded out.

* * *

Hours later, the sound of rustling nearby caused Perri to stir awake from her unconscious slumber. When she lifted up and focused her eyes, she froze upon realizing that she was not alone in the nook.

Just several feet away from her stood a large moose.

He was staring at her cautiously, yet there was a gentle calmness in his eyes. Perri couldn't move. She had heard about moose being in the forest, but she had never encountered one before. They were rare.

She was terrified, but she had a feeling that one was

not going to harm her. She stared back at him, as if to tell him that she was not there to cause any trouble. He was the most majestic looking creature Perri had ever seen. So big and so powerful. It was really incredible to see one up close. Not many people could be that close to a moose–especially out there.

He let out a faint grunt and then lowered himself to the ground. Once he was in a resting position, he kept his head held up and maintained eye contact with Perri. She felt like he was the wisest creature in the universe. And now that she'd been to multiple, maybe he was the wisest creature in *all* the universes.

Something about the look in his eyes gave Perri a sense of hope. It filled her with a surge of optimism. Even more than what she already had, thanks to Dr. Pearson. She felt like that moose had all of the answers. Like he was some all-knowing sage.

"Can you…speak?" Perri reluctantly asked.

The moose looked at her. Unfazed by the words that had just left her mouth.

"Can you understand what I'm saying?"

Again, the moose just looked at her. His expression remained unchanged.

She was starting to feel a bit silly now. Of course he wasn't some all-knowing sage. He was just a moose. A big, majestic, and intimidating creature. Yet one that appeared to be kind and gentle, since she remained unharmed.

Then Perri thought back to that day when she and Evan had come down to the nook. The day they had accidentally crossed into The Haze for the first time. The boat that Evan had hidden there in the nook was missing. It had been dislodged by something that caused it to slide down into the river. They had assumed it was a bear, but it's entirely possible it was the very moose that lay before her.

Perri eyed the moose again. "You're the one that knocked that boat into the river, aren't you?" She studied his expression carefully for the slightest change. Nothing.

"Somehow, some way, it was your fault we got into this whole mess. If that boat would've been right here, we wouldn't have been in the water to begin with. We wouldn't have been sucked in. We'd have never left this universe and we'd have stuck to the plan. We'd be far away from that stupid Haze. And Evan and I would've never gotten separated." She was raising her voice now and getting increasingly hysterical. Which in most cases would've been a big mistake. But the moose still remained unfazed. He was calm. And he kept his still gaze on Perri.

When she was done lashing out at that silent but attentive listener, she realized how much sillier she now felt for yelling at a seemingly innocent moose. He was probably there to simply rest on the cool grass in that shaded nook. And there she was disturbing his peace. She should be thankful that he wasn't trying to trample her.

When she calmed down, the moose slowly got back

up to a looming, standing position. He walked slowly towards Perri, closing the gap that was between them. She backed up until she was against the wall of the nook. The moose stopped. Then he lowered his head in a sort of bow, almost as if indicating he wanted Perri to place her hand on the top of his head. She did. His fur was just as soft and gentle as his personality seemed. Then he lifted his head and his eyes met her gaze for a moment.

Perri felt as though they had some sort of understanding between them. She didn't quite know what it was, though. All she did was accuse him of being something more than a moose and yell at him. All he did was listen to her and not trample her. But something about the look in his eyes really seemed to make her feel hopeful—like all was not lost.

He turned around and started to walk out of the nook. He crossed the river and headed towards the other side of the forest. Before he got too far, Perri called back out to him.

"Hey!"

The moose stopped, but he didn't turn around.

"Have you seen anyone else? I'm trying to find my best friend, Evan. I want to know if he made it back home, too. I don't know if you really are just a moose, or if you know things, or if I'm really losing it now. But I just want to know if you've seen my friend." Perri's voice trailed off, as she felt incredibly ridiculous for talking to a moose. But she was desperate.

The moose turned his head to look at her one last time and then disappeared into the trees.

"What does that mean?" she called back out to him. "Hey! Come back!"

She started to run after him but tripped and fell over a branch. Something sharp dug hard into her thigh and she felt a jolt of pain. She reached into her pocket and found the culprit. It was her DNA tracker.

"I suppose I have no use of you anymore now that I'm home," she said, smiling down at the small metal device.

As she placed it back into her pocket, she heard a short, high-pitched melodic trill that made her heart drop down into her toes.

Her thumb must've been touching the pad. And that tone meant one thing—the device had just displayed the coordinates of her counterpart in this universe.

It meant that she wasn't home after all.

Perri slowly pulled the DNA tracker out of her pocket. Hands trembling. She stared at the coordinates that were on display. Pure agony filled her insides. Then with all of the might she could muster, she chucked the DNA tracker as far as she could into the river.

She never wanted to see it again.

CHAPTER NINETEEN

Perri was done. She was angry. No more games. No more playing around.

She was tired of everything being taken from her. Her home, her memories, her best friend, and now the bit of hope she had just regained. She was tired of it. All of it. Rage welled up inside her like a terrible volcano on the verge of eruption.

She was a prisoner of The Haze. Ever since crossing into it, it had done nothing but torment her. Playing with her like some cruel, mighty being torturing that which it deemed beneath it.

Pure fury filled Perri's innards now. She did not want anything to do with The Haze again. It was nothing but trouble.

She took the imprinter out of her pocket and brought it down hard over her knee. To her surprise, it snapped in half just as if it were a wooden pencil. She fully expected nothing to happen, as the device had appeared to be metal. But she picked up the two halves and chucked them into the river to float away along with the DNA tracker. She did not want the reminder of any of it.

No more.

She decided that it was time to just face the fact that

Evan was gone and she'd never see him again. If she was lucky, maybe there would be a version of him there. But if not, then that's just the way it was. She was not stepping another foot through that Haze.

No more.

She was not giving up. She was fighting back. To her, it seemed as if The Haze wanted her to keep crossing, so that it could keep taking her memories. Keep toying with her. And she was not giving into it. She was done playing its game.

No more.

Trembling with fury, Perri took one final, long-lasting look at The Haze. She remembered all the people she had met along the way there. The doppelganger Evan who had seemed so much different than her own. Maybe there was one in this universe. Maybe not. She thought of Tilly. Her flowing silver robes and her obsession with those light trees. How helpful she had been in making sure Evan and Perri understood what was going on. Tilly was kind and thoughtful. Quirky, as some scientists tended to be.

Then she thought of James. And his wife and daughter. She wondered where they had ended up. Hopefully somewhere safe. Perri supposed the one good thing that came from her time through The Haze was getting to save James and his family. She figured how ironic it was that she now viewed The Haze as some villainous thing, when James and his family had probably strongly revered it. It saved them from that ravaged world they had lived in. Assuming it didn't just transport them to a universe even worse than that one.

Then there was Dr. Pearson. Perri's own doppel-ganger. So much temper, so much loneliness. A life with-out friendship. A life without Evan Miles. But under-neath that temper was the same Perri that she was. Kind and soft. She had let her stay with her. And she had given her hope.

Hope that was of no use. It had led her here. In which she had just met that creature. That moose. What was that all about? He filled her with more hope and more optimism, but he was just an animal. Then he left.

Like everything else. Gone.

Perri took a deep breath and turned away from The Haze. She took off in the direction of the city, trying to decide what to do first. She could either try to investigate her doppelganger, which she now knew existed thanks to the DNA tracker. Or she could see if there was an Evan counterpart. Or she could explore the area to see what was different.

Either way, Perri knew one thing—she was getting tired of the same song and dance routine. She was just tired, period. That's why no matter what, this was going to be her home now. No more Haze. This was it.

During her journey to town, she tried to figure out what memory had been taken from her this time. She went over every major event in her head she could think of. Nothing appeared to be lost. She could remember Evan, obviously. She remembered the orphanage, she remembered college, she remembered work and The

Company. And she clearly seemed to remember the different universes she'd traveled through up to that point. It appeared she had not forgotten anything big. Maybe she'd just lost something small. But that caused her to think on something else.

How would she know what memory was lost if she was unable to remember what she'd forgotten? That made Perri realize the dangers of going through The Haze alone. She couldn't imagine what would have happened if she'd made the whole journey without Evan.

Perri still couldn't help but wonder where he was. She liked to think that after the blast, he had gotten right back up and into The Haze. And that he was just living in some universe with some version of herself. It made her somewhat sad and somewhat jealous. But it was better than thinking he was dead. She refused to believe that he was dead.

Maybe that's what was meant for them. To wind up in universes where there were counterparts that needed them. Maybe Evan was in a universe with a very distraught Perri that needed him. And maybe somewhere in this universe was a doppelganger of Evan that needed Perri. If that was how things were supposed to be, then so be it. She decided that it wasn't the worst way for their story to end.

Upon arriving in town, Perri realized that it looked almost identical to her universe. Almost down to every single chip and crack in the sidewalk that ran in front of the shops. She made her way to the library so that she could use the computer to search for the doppelgangers.

Having calmed down a bit during her trek from the forest, Perri now felt a bit regretful for tossing the DNA tracker. She could not remember the coordinates that it had displayed. Instead, she searched her name in the city records. Then she realized where the coordinates would've lead her to. The cemetery. It appeared that in this universe, rather than her mother dying during childbirth, Perri was the one that had died. She also learned that her mother had given birth to another child not long after this version of Perri had died. And her parents were both still alive and living in the same city.

That information made Perri feel happy. Happy to know that she was in a universe where her parents were alive and well. She wasn't sure how yet, but someday she would find a way to bump into them. To see them.

As she was pondering the thought of meeting her long-dead parents, Perri heard a bit of commotion from the front of the library. She heard the clerks apparently telling someone they needed to leave. Then she heard the person plead with them to allow him to stay for a bit.

When she heard the voice, her heart lurched and her head spun around so fast she thought she broke her neck.

From a distance, she spotted something orange. The man's hair. It was orange.

She couldn't get a good look at him from the distance she was at. When she got up to move closer, it was too late. The man lost his battle with the clerks as he was being escorted out.

Perri sprinted to the door, and when she made it outside, she looked both directions to see where he went. She spotted him in the distance on her right and yelled after him.

"Evan!"

He turned around, and Perri could make out from the distance that he didn't quite look like her Evan. But after he looked at her, he turned back around and tore out running. Perri went full speed ahead to try to catch up with him.

"Evan, wait!"

He wouldn't slow down. He wouldn't turn around. Perri was gaining on him, as he looked like he was very weak from exhaustion. Then she saw him drop down and disappear under a nearby bridge.

As she was about to make the same drop, someone called out to her.

"You might as well give up, lady," said the stranger.

Perri looked behind her and saw an older woman standing outside a nearby shop, which she appeared to own.

"He's the town bum. And he sure is a weirdo, if you ask me. Always going around from shop to shop, place to place. Asking to just sit for a while. People have tried to help him, ya know. But he lives under that bridge. He won't take help from anyone. And he runs from everyone that tries. People are tired of it. And he smells. No one wants that in their business. And you can't blame them."

Perri didn't say anything. She just looked at the lady

and nodded with a smile. The lady shook her head and went back into her shop.

Perri slowly walked over to the bridge and peered over. She saw him sitting down there in a heap of blankets. He was huddled all by himself. All she could see was the top of his head. That dark orange hair.

"Evan," Perri called down to him.

"Go away, ma'am," he said curtly. "I don't know how you know my name. But just forget it. Take that lady's advice and give up. She's right. I won't take help from anyone. So, just leave me alone." Then he looked up at her. Perri noticed an emptiness in those navy blue eyes. A sadness. And his face was filthy. Almost completely covered in black dots and marks from who knows what. He moved his gaze back to his little abode and said nothing.

Perri backed away from the bridge. She continued her thought from earlier.

The Evan she had just encountered needed her. She had ended up in a universe with a doppelganger version of her best friend that was in terrible shape. And with her help, she could change his life. Maybe that's what all the hope was about. All the hope that Dr. Pearson had given her. All the hope and optimism she had felt from that moose encounter. It wasn't about finding her Evan, it was about finding this one. She was being selfish, when really there was a version of him out there that needed her. Here he was.

She still missed her Evan so much. Even more so now that she had just come into contact with this one.

After seeing his face, his hair, his eyes. Hearing his voice. She missed him. All she hoped for now was that he had experienced what she just did. The realization that he was needed by a version of her.

Wanting to know what had happened to cause this Evan to turn out that way, Perri made her way back to the library to do some research. If this universe was that similar to her own, then maybe there was a version of The Company that was even worse. Maybe it had a much stronger hold and it had destroyed Evan's life somehow.

Nope. To her relief, there appeared to be no record of The Company in this city or anywhere in this universe.

Then she wondered if he still lost his parents. If so, going to the orphanage and not having a version of Perri there probably would've done him in. That's probably what had caused him to be that way. Assuming he had the same personality as her Evan. Which, by the looks of it, wouldn't surprise her.

When she searched his name in the city records, the results made no sense to her, so she searched again.

And again.

And again.

She thought there was a mistake. But clearly, there must not have been. She searched a hundred times before finally accepting what she had read.

Evan's family still had their bad car accident. But his parents and his little brother weren't killed in the accident.

He was.

Evan had died at the age of eight. He was the only casualty in the accident. His parents and brother were still alive.

That meant...the Evan living under the bridge. The one Perri had just spoken to. He wasn't a doppelganger from this universe.

It was Evan. THE Evan. Her Evan.

Perri couldn't breathe. The room was spinning.

She nearly knocked the computer over when she rose up from the desk. Losing her balance, she tripped before getting back to her feet and sprinting out the door. She ran as fast as she could back to that bridge. Not wasting any time to look over the edge, she just jumped over without hesitation. That startled Evan, as he let out a short yell.

Perri looked into his eyes. His navy blue eyes. She focused on his hair. His dark orange, unkempt hair. Tears filled her eyes.

She threw her arms around him and squeezed Evan in a tight embrace. He was standing still, eyes wide, unsure of what was going on. Perri pulled back and noticed that the black dots and marks all over his face weren't from dirt or filth. She noticed he had markings all over his neck. Then she pulled up his sleeves and saw that his arms were completely covered in markings.

Tally marks. All over. Not just the underside of his wrist. Everywhere.

"Pete," Perri said, voice shaking. "What have you done?"

Evan stared at her. "Who are you?"

CHAPTER TWENTY

"Why do you keep following me?" Evan continued. "And why won't you leave me alone?"

Perri was silent. Staring melancholically at the face that had once belonged to her best friend. Whoever that was in front of her no longer knew who she was. And she had an idea as to why, based off the sheer number of marks all over his skin. Assuming he had marked himself every time he'd crossed into The Haze, then it must have finally happened.

He'd forgotten her.

The air felt cold, and she felt the hairs stand up on the back of her neck.

"You really don't know who I am?" Perri asked.

Evan shook his head. "No. I don't. You seem familiar and all, but I don't know much of anything, anyway. So, it's no use." He grabbed his head and sulked back down into his pile of blankets on the ground.

Perri got down on the ground in front of him. "What happened to you?"

Evan looked up at her. He was reluctant at first, but after studying her for a minute he finally responded. "I don't know. Not really. I woke up in the forest near here with a really terrible pain in my head. I didn't know what was going on. Couldn't remember anything. No one was around. So, I walked until I found the nearest place, which was this city. And I've been here ever since. I don't even know how long ago that was. I can't remember anything. All I had was this backpack." He pointed to the corner where a tattered looking leather backpack sat on the ground.

"There are things in there I don't understand. This place feels familiar to me, but I just can't seem to…figure anything out. I've tried going to places around here to see if I can jog my memory. See if anything comes back. But nothing helps. Only thing that seems to remain is my name. Evan. I found it written on something in the backpack and I assumed it was my name. And then when you started calling me that name, I assumed it must be correct." Then his tone changed from one of sadness and gloom to one of suspicion. "That leads me back to MY question, which you still haven't answered. Who are you?"

Perri considered everything Evan had just told her. Of course this place would feel familiar because it's almost identical to their universe, but it wasn't their universe. It still wasn't home. But it was as close as they'd get. And as far as she knew, there was no way to get their memories back. But Evan didn't know that. Granted, she didn't even know that for sure. It just didn't seem likely. The hard truth seemed to be that whatever had been taken from them could never be returned.

Then Perri turned her gaze upon the backpack. She wondered what was inside. The backpack felt familiar to her. She knew she had seen it before. But she couldn't quite place it. It's almost as if there was a hole in her mind where the memory of it was. Maybe that's what The Haze took from her this time. Whatever that backpack was and whatever was inside of it, she'd forgotten about. And now she was eager to reach inside.

She looked back over at Evan, who was still staring at her with a piercing gaze of suspicion. As she was about to open her mouth to respond to him, he stood up swiftly.

"You know what? Forget it. I don't even care who you are. I don't need you. I don't need anyone around here. I'm fine on my own." Tears filled his eyes. "You obviously don't know what it's like to not know who you are. I'm leaving to go find answers, like I've been doing every day. On my own. I don't want to see you here when I get back."

Evan hoisted himself up out of his hideout and took off. Perri started after him, but he called back and told her not to follow him. In a morose manner, Evan went off down the sidewalk alone as she just stood there watching.

Perri couldn't believe what she was seeing. It sent a pang of guilt and heartbreak right through her chest. Seeing her best friend like that was a massive blow. She wished it was her going through it instead of him. He didn't deserve to go through it. He'd gone through so much in his life already—losing his family, the depression and toll that had taken on him, then moving into an orphanage. Granted, they were fortunate enough to have had a good experience there. But because of his issues and his constant clinging to Perri, he had never wanted to be adopted or fostered. So, he had never gotten to experience another family. All he'd had was Perri. Then he had gone through school and struggled to decide what to do there. Then The Company. He'd hated every minute of that. Then they'd stumbled into The Haze.

Evan didn't deserve to lose everything. Or maybe he did, Perri thought. Maybe he deserved a fresh start.

She felt her eyes water, thinking of her friend. How different he was from the person who was memory-less here. But they're not different, they're the same person. It was Evan, but it wasn't.

Perri dropped back down into the hideout and turned back towards the backpack sitting in the corner. Wondering what was inside. She reached for it and opened it up.

She saw only two things sitting inside. His imprinter and a steel box of some sort that appeared to be covered with notes. There also seemed to be a lock on the front of the box. She looked around to make sure no one was lurking nearby and, especially, to make sure Evan wasn't coming right back. Then she reached her hand in the bag and pulled out the locked box.

It was a small cube and didn't feel very heavy as she picked it up and held it in her hands. She noticed a carving on the top that said "From EJM to PJP." The notes written on all sides of the cube appeared to say the same thing over and over. "Evan. Whatever you do, do not lose this and do not open this." The lock that stood in the way between her and whatever contents were hidden away inside the mysterious cube required a four-letter word.

If the cube was truly meant for her, as it surely seemed that way, then she had an idea what the word was. If that really was the Evan she knew, the Evan she grew up with, her best friend in the world, then it could only be one thing.

"Pete."

As she clicked each letter into the lock, she grew more nervous by the millisecond, wondering what in the world could be inside the little cube. "What could Evan have possibly put in this thing for me?"

After the last "E" was entered, she pulled down on the lock and, sure enough, it gave way and disengaged. She removed it from the latch and opened up the cube. To her surprise, the only thing inside the box was a tiny display that showed the words "Play Memo."

She backed up and planted herself firmly down onto the pile of blankets. Perri swallowed a big nervous gulp of air and then she tapped the display. Her eyes widened as she immediately heard Evan's voice come pouring out of the little cube, filling the hideout.

She felt her chest tighten.

"Perri. I'm so sorry. We really got ourselves into a mess, didn't we? Well, I did at least. I think I've been crossing too many times, Pete. You should see me. All the markings I've already got. It's an absolute mess. I'm an absolute mess. I don't even really know where or how to begin this thing. I think it's only been a day or two since we were separated, but it feels like it's been decades. I'm lost

without you. You're my compass, my lighthouse, always guiding me where I needed to go. And you're also my anchor when I lose control of my emotions. I've gone off the rails since being without you, Pete. And I realized just how badly I get on without you. And it's rough. Right after the blast, when I saw you disappear through The Haze, I was blown backwards. But The Haze pulled me right in before another blast hit. I must have crossed a dozen times that first hour, frantically searching for you. I started to quickly lose count of how many times I was crossing because I was doing it so rapidly. I was frantic. I didn't care where I was. I ran and searched for you, and if I didn't see you in the vicinity, I went back through. And I did it over and over and over. Between the massive headaches and the increasing memory loss, I started slowing down. I crossed so many times, Pete. So many. I finally stopped to think about what memories I had left. To try to focus on them and hold onto what I could. If I could."

Evan's voice stopped, and after several seconds of silence, Perri noticed the display now showed the word "Next." When she tapped it, a new recording started to play as Evan's voice once again filled the hideout.

"It's funny when you think about it, Pete. All I ever wanted to do was just get away from that horrible life of ours. Run away. That's what I wanted more than anything. I hated that place so much. And then you finally started hating it, too. But, you see, the best part about my life was you. I never wanted to get away from you, Perri."

The word "Next" once again flashed on the display

to indicate there was another recording available. Perri could feel her eyes water every time she heard Evan's voice. She could hear the pain in his words. Her hands were trembling as she reached out to tap the display again.

"We never should have run away, Pete. I should've finally told you what I wanted to tell you for years. What I wanted to tell you that day of your bad accident. I know you don't remember it. But what I wanted to tell you that day and every day since is that you're my everything. I wouldn't be who I am without you. I should've told you a long time ago how I've always felt. Then instead of running away, we could've just lived better lives where we were. I should have listened to you, as always. We had that choice all along to make our lives better, but I was too afraid. I was too focused on us running away and getting out of there. Look where it got us. We're literally worlds apart now. And it's all my fault. I did this to us, Pete. And I'm so sorry."

Perri's heart pounded as she tapped "Next."

"Perri, I have crossed so many times that I can barely even remember our home. I can barely remember anything. I can feel it all slipping away. Little by little. I feel myself changing. I've been fighting so hard just to keep you in my mind and I fear that crossing through one more time is going to cause me to lose you, too. But I just...I have to try. I can't give up. I just can't. I won't. I'll find my way back to you, Perri. I'm recording this because I just wanted to feel like I was talking to you again. And to have that small bit of hope that if I don't find you, then

maybe you'll find me. You were always the smartest and strongest of the two of us anyway. I think I'll have to leave myself notes in case I lose the memory of you altogether. But I'll keep this recording safe and locked away. In the hopes that one day, one way or another, we will find each other again."

After tapping "Next," Perri could feel a sort of finality in the tone of Evan's voice now emanating from the cube.

"I'm gonna have to load up and head to The Haze again, Pete. I have to. Maybe this time will be the one. We really shouldn't have run away. I'd give anything to just go back to our old lives. The good and the bad. With you there, I know I could've survived the bad. You outweighed it. I'm sorry for everything, Pete. For once in my life, I want to finally tell you the thing I've waited too long to say. The one thing I know that can never be erased from my mind or my heart. And that's how I feel. Perri, I love you."

Perri stared at the display, hoping to see another "Next" pop up. But it was just blank. She tapped it furiously yet nothing happened. Perri's eyes were so full of tears that they began to overflow and stream down her face as she stared at the cube clutched in her grasp.

"I love you too, Evan," Perri choked out. "Pete. Perri and Evan Together Eternally."

She thought of that little boy she had met in the orphanage all those years ago. With his orange, untidy hair and his navy blue eyes. Perri's best friend that she'd grown up with. Her feelings were just the same. She'd always wanted to tell him, but she'd never had the courage. She thought of his laugh and his smile.

The realization finally set in that her Evan, in a sense, had died. While he wasn't literally dead, the person he was, the memories, the personality, all of that was gone.

Perri sobbed, clutching the cube.

She closed the lid and reopened it. Then the words "Play Memo" reappeared on the display. After replaying Evan's messages a couple of times, Perri finally closed the cube and replaced the lock. Then she put it back inside the backpack. She wiped her eyes and composed herself.

It was hard for her to comprehend exactly how to move forward. Then she remembered her hope. Her optimism. Just earlier, she had been thinking this was a doppelganger Evan and that she was meant to help him. Well, it turned out that it was not a doppelganger Evan. But she was still meant to help him after all. She wasn't going anywhere. And neither was he. He was searching for answers, and while he may never find them, at least she was there now.

Like Evan said, Perri was always his light. His way out of darkness. She could help him. And he needed her now more than ever.

Perri had seen a glimpse of what her life might be like without Evan when she had seen Dr. Pearson. She needed Evan, too. They balanced each other out.

Perri climbed out of Evan's hideout and decided to try to search for him. She scoured all over town trying to find him. She remembered the strange lady from before telling her that he liked to just go sit for a while wherever he went. Perri got the idea to start looking for any of the areas where there were benches.

After a couple hours of searching, she finally spotted him from a distance, sitting on a bench next to a tree. It reminded her of a spot from their childhood. The spot where the name "Pete" was born. As she stood just watching him from a distance, she thought about what must have been going through his head. How confused he must be. Not knowing who he was or where he was. She only felt a little tiny piece of that with the gaps in her memory.

They were incredibly fortunate. Just earlier, she had been filled with so much rage that she thought she would explode. But now, there she stood, just feet away from Evan.

Reunited at last. Sure, not in the way they'd thought, but reunited at last.

From the start, Evan and Perri had wanted to run away. She still could no longer remember what had specifically prompted them to want to run. But they'd both apparently deemed their old lives so bad that they'd wanted to leave them and start over in a new place.

Well, there they were. In a new place. Starting over. Just like they'd wanted.

Though not exactly like they'd wanted. But things worked out. Hope was not lost. She had tried to remain as positive as possible during all the hardships. She had failed a few times but then was lifted back up. Thanks to

Dr. Pearson. Thanks to that moose. She didn't lose hope. Things had happened the way they did for whatever reason. But she supposed it all worked out better than it could have otherwise.

Perri took a deep breath, knowing the next few steps she took were going to begin the rest of her life.

She shook off the nerves she was feeling, then walked towards the orange-haired man who was sitting on the bench, staring down at the ground.

"Hey, kid!" yelled Perri from a few feet away.

Evan looked up from the ground and saw Perri walking towards him. His eyes were red and watery, as if he'd just been crying.

She stopped right in front of him. "What's your name, kid?"

He looked at her with a puzzled expression on his face before slowly answering, "Evan."

"It's great to meet you, Evan. I'm Perri Pearson." She sat down next to him and looked him in the eyes. "Look, kid. Things are going to be tough for a little while. You've just lost a lot. But the thing is, so have I. You've cried. I've cried. It's okay. But trust me, it's going to get better."

Evan gave her a hint of a smile, and a little glow seemed to appear behind his navy blue eyes.

Perri stood back up in front of him and held out her hand. "Trust me, Evan. Everything is going to be okay. Just stick with me and I'll look after you. You'll be in great hands." Perri winked at Evan and flashed a big cheesy grin. Evan smiled back and chuckled. "Now come on, let's have a look around this place. It's new to me, too, but I have a feeling it won't be so bad once we get used to it."

Evan reached out and grabbed Perri's hand, and together they headed off to explore this new world they would call home.

THE END

ACKNOWLEDGMENTS

First and foremost, I owe many thanks to my wife, Jaysie. Not only for being subjected to various readings of the many stages of this story, but also for taking on the arduous task of editing this work, as she and I both know that I was a bit of a nag during our back-and-forths. (Sorry, honey. But I couldn't have done this without you. You're the best.)

I also need to give a big shout-out to two of my great friends who provided me with invaluable feedback and insight when provided with an early draft of this story. Samantha Van Meter and Lauren Riggs, my sincere thanks to the both of you.

I owe a great deal of thanks to the many people who have read my first work, Mr. Travels, and expressed their kind words to me. Without that support and those words of encouragement, I would not be able to continue writing with the passion and the excitement that I feel. Thank you to you all.

Lastly, I want to thank my wife again along with all my friends and especially my family. Without all of their love and support, I wouldn't be where I am today, with the ability to do what I do. The encouragement they have given me during my writing is something that cannot be measured. But it is certainly most appreciated and this book couldn't have happened without it.